# A Heart Behind Enemy Lines

Elisabeth Constantino

# About the author

Having a degree in Publicity from Mackenzie Presbyterian University and graduate studies in communications from the Superior School of Adverting and Marketing (ESPM, acronym in Portuguese), the author has worked in the area in various national and multinational companies for over ten years.

She spent over a year in Manchester, United Kingdom, working and studying. It was in England that she took her first literary steps.

In 2014, health issues forced her to leave her main job in Marketing, dedicating herself exclusively to her literary work, the novel *A Heart Behind Enemy Lines*.

The author currently works in the area of communications and has developed plans for a new literary project.

# DEDICATION

I dedicate this book to my family. They have always supported me in victory and defeat. I am, especially thankful for the warm reception I received by the British family who opened their doors to me, during my stay in England, where I was able to experience the European climate and lifestyle that motivated me to write this book.

## Table of contents

Chapter I ................................................................ 2
Chapter II ............................................................... 6
Chapter III .............................................................. 9
Chapter IV ............................................................. 17
Chapter V .............................................................. 22
Chapter VI ............................................................. 26
Chapter VII ............................................................ 35
Chapter VIII ........................................................... 41
Chapter IX ............................................................. 46
Chapter X .............................................................. 51
Chapter XI ............................................................. 77
Chapter XII ........................................................... 100
Chapter XIII .......................................................... 108
Chapter XIV .......................................................... 120
Chapter XV ........................................................... 129
Chapter XVI .......................................................... 139
Chapter XVII ......................................................... 151
Chapter XVIII ........................................................ 156
Chapter XIX .......................................................... 163
Chapter XX ........................................................... 170
Chapter XXI .......................................................... 181
Chapter XXII ......................................................... 196
Chapter XXIII ........................................................ 207

Chapter XXIV ............................................................. 213
Chapter XXV .............................................................. 221

# Chapter I

It's been six months since Jane has had any contact with her father, Colonel John Myer. The threat of war has been echoing all across Europe. Her father, one of the most important men in the Royal Army, is on many of the main committees dealing with war, which makes their seeing each other again even more difficult.

The only child of a highly respected family and surrounded by every possible material comfort, Jane has grown up around books while at her mother's side. She's had little contact with the society near her, just as there are no friends in her life. Her mother, Margaret Myer, has always been concerned about her daughter's seclusion and isolation, but that didn't bother Jane, who felt complete with her books and with all the comforts provided by her social status.

Her father, although physically absent, wrote her frequently and his affection for her was visible to everyone.

"I really miss my father!", Jane exclaims, sighing, reading the latest letter from him.

"Settle down, dear! He said he's on his way home in his letter, remember? We'll see him soon!" Margaret responds, while affectionately hugging her daughter.

"He mentioned in it that he's bringing fantastic news. Could it be that there won't be another war?" Jane wonders, delicately pushing her mother away, who'd been hugging her tightly at the moment.

"He also wrote that to me, my dear, but I don't think they've solved the problem of the war; if they had, we would've heard about in on the radio. It must be something else!" Margaret adds, sitting down in her rocking chair in the garden.

Winter was coming to an end. The snow that had covered the ground was no longer visible and today the sun was out in all its splendor.

Jane had always loved taking long walks in her city's woods. She felt like a caged bird when winter arrived and kept her from going out.

On those walks, she cherished both nature and her books sitting on the grass in the shade of a tree to read. Jane's reading habits were varied, without preferences; what enchanted her was knowledge, which she readily acquired.

English literature fascinated her, but her desire to learn indubitably sparked her interest in other languages.

"Someday I'm going to learn French fluently and read Alexandre Dumas's adventures in their original language, without any adaptations!" Jane exclaimed.

A week had gone by since her father's last letter. Jane was now anxious to hear his good news, when she noticed considerable commotion in front of her home.

Curious and excited, she ran down the main staircase, asking "Is it Dad?" with a smile.

The governess waiting for her at the foot of the stares confirmed her doubts.

"It doesn't matter if you're ten or 18, you'll still run down the stairs! You know that's very dangerous!" her governess says, shaking her head worriedly.

"You're always watching out for me, aren't you, Nana?" That was, the affectionate nickname Jane had given her governess in homage of the book *Peter Pan*. Nana had taken care of Jane since she was little. Thanks to her, Jane's passion for literature had begun.

She was opening the front door when her father enters accompanied by her mother.

"Dad, I've missed you so much!", Jane exclaimed, hugging her father tightly.

"This time, stay with us for at least six months, please?" Jane asks, in a childlike and excited voice.

"This time, I'll be with you much longer than that," says Col. Myer, hugging his wife and daughter simultaneously.

"Did you leave the Army? Is there no longer a threat of war? Has Germany reached an agreement?" Jane asks, euphorically.

Before Jane could ask him anything else, Col. Myer cover's Jane's mouth with his hand and answers, "No, my pumpkin. Unfortunately, there's still a threat of war and I'm still in the army, but the good news is that I'm being sent to work at a British base in Germany and I can take my family with me, since there's no prospect of returning soon. So, it's good news because I can work with you at my side!" Col. Myer exclaims.

"Dear, wouldn't it be very dangerous to take the family to a British base in Germany right now?" Margaret asks, concerned.

"I hesitated at first, dear, but they guaranteed me the base has been installed in a safe and very protected area. Up until now, the Germans have peacefully accepted our presence in that region, which is why other army families are already there." John pauses briefly and the happiness in his face is overcome by concern. "But if you don't go, it'll be the end of me. I might not be able to come home for years if our diplomacy with Germany fails," John adds with an air of concern.

"Well, Mum!" Jane exclaims, stepping between her parents. "I'm sure nothing bad's going to happen to us. The Germans must know about Col. John Myer's wrath," Jane playfully asserts, resulting in a collective laugh.

The next morning, Jane and her mother begin the process of moving.

In the following month, all preparations for the move are duly organized and Jane and her family sadly say goodbye to their home.

"Bye, my home. See you in a few years!" Jane says longingly. She's the last one to enter the car.

# Chapter II

Jane was on the transport ship, contemplating the nature surrounding her and all of its details.

"What are you doing, dear?" John asks. He'd been watching her from afar.

"I'm starting a diary, Dad! I want to describe all of our time on the base! Who knows, somebody might use my notes someday and write a book…"

"Why don't you write it yourself?! After all, I don't know any young lady who's more articulate and well-read than you," John asked Jane, who now was wandering about in her daydreams.

"What could I write? Maybe about some adventure in the Bavarian Alps, maybe an action piece about a modern knight's adventures… that's a book Don Quixote would appreciate!"

Without realizing it, she began smiling to herself, worrying her father, who began asking her questions.

"Maybe you've been out in the sun too long, don't you think? Why don't we go inside and keep your mother company?"

Both head toward the deck, when one of the sailor's intercepts Col. Myer.

"We'll dock within an hour, sir. Is there anything you need for your family?"

"No, seaman, we're fine. Please ask the captain if we'll be able to reach the base before sunset."

"Are you afraid of something, Dad? You seem worried!" Jane inquires, putting her hand on his shoulder.

"I don't like the idea of travelling with you two in this region after dark. Don't worry, my child. We'll be at our new home soon."

It was a little after six in the evening when the ship docked in German territory. Col. Myer rushed to get his family off the ship.

Upon arriving at the base, Jane was fascinated by her new home. The house was one of the most beautiful on the base, surrounded by duly uniformed guards carrying weapons, ready for action.

Jane was young and had never experienced anything negative in her life, like, for example, the universe of war with all of its violent nuances. She knew war was bad, and that people died, but nothing beyond that was part of her world.

Since Jane was a beautiful, blue-eyed young woman, as soon as she entered the base, all of the soldiers' eyes turned toward her. They were instantly reprimanded by Col. Myer, who, with his authoritarian voice, ordered, "Atten-TION!"

The soldiers all obeyed his command, fascinating Jane even more with everyone's movement and obedience.

"Yes, my dear. I love soldiers, too. Isn't that obvious?" Margaret asked. Smiling, she held onto her husband's arm.

Entering the house, Jane noticed she wasn't the only young woman there. In spite of seeming very large from the outside, the house was small inside because it held so many families.

"I thought this would be all ours," says Jane, with a sad expression.

"This is our home, dear, but the families of other high-ranking officers are also living here," John responds, affectionately caressing his daughter's long, straight chestnut locks. "Look how many young girls, there are your age. You'll soon make friends with them!"

With her father's words, Jane felt a chill run down her spine.

"Friends?" Jane thinks. "I wonder if they like to read."

She was very nervous and didn't feel well in the presence of so many people. Reclusive, she attended few social events; she wasn't comfortable being around so many people.

Struggling with her own anxieties, Jane went up the house's main staircase and, with the help of her father, entered her quarters.

"At least the room is just mine!" Jane exclaimed, smiling, throwing herself on her new and comfortable bed.

# Chapter III

Jane woke up a little late the next morning. She was tired from the voyage.

Descending the stairs, she found her mother deep in conversation with a circle of women.

"Jane, dear, is this any time for a young woman to wake up? The day's half over and you were still sleeping!" Margaret says in a firm voice.

Concerned about having gotten up so late, she looks for a clock to see what time it is.

"Mum, it's nine o'clock!" she exclaims, kissing her sweetly on the forehead.

Since everyone had already left, Jane has breakfast by herself that morning. She never saw solitude as a problem, because she enjoyed every instant of it to her great satisfaction.

Returning to the main lobby, Jane finds her mother again with the same group. This time, Margaret presents her to them.

"This is my daughter, Jane!" Margaret says proudly.

"Your daughter's beautiful! A little short for her age, but she's a lovely young lady!" one of the women announces in a mischievous tone.

"Nothing that can't be compensated for with shoes and the right clothes!" suggests another, meticulously eyeing Jane over.

"My daughter lives with us in the country and has few friends. We preferred tutoring her at home rather than sending her to school. We were afraid my husband's profession would interfere with her wellbeing," Margaret responds, a little embarrassed by her daughter's clothes.

Margaret gently and subtly guides her daughter to her room.

"We should get you some new cloths; you're a colonel's daughter. You can't go about poorly dressed!" Margaret says, looking over all of Jane's clothes.

"What's wrong with my clothes, Mum? We bought new clothes for the trip, remember?" Jane asks, trying to calm her mother down and impeding her frenetic search.

"My child, I don't want those women gossiping about my family. They think I have no class, that we're "bumpkins" … so jealous, just jealous!" Margaret repeats, blushing.

Jane smiles and kisses her mother, but she thinks such concerns are foolish. She then takes out a book to read near the window.

"What are you doing?" Margaret asks.

"I thought I'd read a little, to relax," Jane answers, with the book already covering her face, trying to avoid her mother.

"You'll go downstairs this very minute and get acquainted with those girls," Margaret orders, taking Jane's book. "That's not a request, young lady. You've been a stick in the mud long enough! How do you intend to find a husband that way?" Margaret pulls Jane from her chair. Before she realizes what's happening, her mother changes her daughter's dress, putting a newer one on her.

Jane's startled by her mother's tone of voice and sudden attitude. She realizes that her life was about to change forever. Obeying her mother, she puts on prettier and more expensive, but uncomfortable pair of shoes and leaves her room with her eyes brimming with tears she can't control.

After departing her room, Jane pulls herself together near the stairs and, decided to face her fear, descends the staircase.

At the foot of the stairs, she's approached by a group of girls who, taking her arms, say, "Welcome!"

Jane is startled by the strength of the group's exclamation, but smiles and answers more softly, "Thanks. My name's Jane."

She quickly observes the girls and begins to understand what had been wrong with her clothes. Jane was wearing neither makeup, a short dress, nor high heels, and had done little with her hair. "Those girls are beautiful!", she thinks.

"Have you been shown around the base?" one of them asks Jane.

"No, I got here yesterday and …"

Before she could finish her sentence, the girls pull her outside.

Now outdoors, Jane notices one of the most beautiful things she's seen in her entire life: a beautiful alp nearby. Because it's spring, flowers cover the peak, exuding a delicious aroma she tries to identify.

"Let's go to the base center. If we leave now, we should get there before the soldiers finish training!" one of the girls proposes, tugging on Jane.

"Soldiers? With this scenery, they want to see soldiers?" Jane thinks, letting herself be carried along by the group while trying to still see the landscape.

"Jane, how old are you?" one of the girls, apparently the oldest in the group, asks.

"I'm 18. Excuse me, but… what are your names?" Jane asks somewhat awkwardly.

"My…! How rude, girls! I'm Sarah, that's Debby, the skinny one's Tina, and that one ahead, the one in a hurry, is Agatha!" responds the oldest girl.

Jane isn't interested in her new companions' ages. It doesn't make much difference since, with makeup, they all looked like women.

Reaching the base's center, Jane encounters a square with flowers sporting a huge English flag in the center guarded by two soldiers.

"There they are!" shouts Agatha, pointing at a field behind the square.

All of the girls run to the field, including Jane, who didn't want to get lost.

Approaching the field, the girls pull mirrors and makeup from their purses to cover up their perspiration from running.

Sarah notices that Jane isn't wearing any makeup and offers her red lipstick.

"No thanks, that's not necessary," Jane says, pushing Sarah's hand away from her face, as if what Sarah was offering were toxic.

"Are you sure you don't want to add a little color to that pallid face? The soldiers might thing you're sick," Sarah asks.

Sarah's words make the other girls giggle.

"Maybe that's Jane's plan, Sarah. The soldiers walk by and she faints. Then they all take her to the sickbay," Debby says, smiling.

"I wonder if that'll work," Agatha asks, now thinking about removing her makeup.

"That's not it... I just don't feel right with makeup," Jane responds in a serious tone, which makes the other girls stop chuckling.

"Let's go, girls, leave the greenhorn behind!" Tina exclaims, winking at Jane. "The guys will be here shortly, and we need to concentrate on this!"

Jane smiles at Tina to thank her but, in her mind, she doesn't understand. "Soldiers... concentrate on this... why?"

Even though Jane clearly understands these girls' objectives, she doesn't understand why she's been put in that context. Her values and priorities don't fit in this scene; nevertheless, not knowing the way back to her "home", she lets herself get dragged along for the moment as a mere observer.

Every morning, soldiers gather on the parade ground for physical activities, like running or squat thrusts, among others. At eleven o'clock, they return to their barracks to get ready for lunch and for their next activities, obeying orders from their superiors.

It was their return to the barracks that interested the girls the most, since the parade grounds had only one exit, which is why they positioned themselves next to it, hoping to be seen.

"There's nothing more gorgeous than shirtless soldiers, is there, Debby?" Agatha asks.

"Certainly not!" Debby smiles.

"Why are we waiting here?" Jane inquires.

"What do you mean 'why'?" Sarah asks with a grin. "Isn't the view here perfectly clear?"

"I thought you were going to show me the base?" Jane asks anxiously, uncomfortable with the whole situation.

"This is the base, Jane!" Sarah responds, pointing at the soldiers.

They all smile broadly after Sarah's comment, except for Jane, who decides to sit by a tree and pulls a small diary from her bra.

"What am I going to write here? This is the most awkward moment in my entire life," Jane thinks, now isolated from the group.

The girls don't notice Jane's brief disappearance. It's eleven o'clock and the soldiers are approaching.

"Good morning, my little pretties!" a shirtless soldier shouts in greeting, winking at all of them.

"Good morning, lads!" they all exclaim in unison, except for Jane who, observes the scene from afar.

"It's always good to have a quality audience here!" the shirtless soldier confirms, nearing the girls.

They all smile and offer the soldier their hands, who promptly kisses them all. He then calls some friends who join the group with the same glee.

Jane decides not to pay any more attention to the group and calmly begins writing in her diary.

After a few minutes, the laughter intensifies, disturbing Jane, who can no longer concentrate on her diary.

"I want to go back to England!" Jane thinks, with a small tear in her eyes.

They hear a bell ring in the distance, which makes the soldiers leave the girls and run to their barracks.

"Such a pity… bloody war!" Agatha exclaims, kicking a small rock on the ground.

Without the soldiers and their flirting, Sarah now wonders where Jane had been, since she was approaching the group.

"Shall we see the base now?" Jane asks, pointing toward a lovely water fountain that she'd been observing from the distance.

"We don't have time, Jane," Tina responds. "We need to get back for lunch or we'll be given a warning."

Jane follows her new friends back to the house with deep sadness.

# Chapter IV

The girls arrive at the mansion a little past one. Following standing orders, a soldier on duty notifies Col. Myer that his daughter has returned.

"What's this, Jane? Returning for lunch at this time?" John asks her, rather irritated.

"Father, I went with the girls to see the base and…"

Before Jane could finish her sentence, using his command voice, the colonel barks, "Jane Myer, I don't care who you were with or where you were… A well-brought-up young lady knows full well when meals are served and will not put herself on display in unknown places. If your friends aren't familiar with schedules, it's up to you to educate them."

Finishing, Col. Myer was flushed and his loud, authoritarian voice frightened Jane, who began to cry.

"You've never yelled at me before," Jane says, using her hands to wipe away the profusion of tears covering her face.

"I'm sorry, my child. Your old man just wants what's best for you. We're in enemy territory, facing a potential war. I really worry about you and your mother," the colonel responds.

"I thought you said the base was safe!" Jane says, rather worried.

"Yes, pumpkin, it is. Nevertheless, we don't know how long our negotiations will be friendly. Honestly, I'm thinking about sending you and your mother back to England." Col. Myer is pale and carries his hand to his mouth, worried.

"Father, we've only been here a day and I'm still tired from the trip. Are you sure we should leave?" Jane asks, now hugging her father.

"I don't know… in the meeting this morning…" Col. Myer realizes that he's frightening his daughter and does not complete his thought. "Go inside immediately and spend the afternoon here at home, with your mother. That's not a request!"

Jane, realizing how very worried her father is, runs into the house and joins the girls, who were now eating a late lunch.

"I think Jane just got her first scolding," Sarah commented, with a smirk on her face.

"Dad's right. It's very dangerous to not follow the base's rules. I should've been more responsible," Jane insists, taking her seat at the table.

"Our parents are complicated. They demand that we marry well but don't want us dating… it's absurd. I'm not a POW", Agatha vented, shouting the last part.

"Careful, Agatha! You'll get us all in trouble," Debby says, covering Agatha's mouth.

"My father doesn't want me to leave the house this afternoon," Jane states, without looking at her friends.

"Jane, sweetie, if we stay home, we'll wilt," Tina comments, grinning.

"Moving on, this morning, I heard my father telling some soldiers that the British base is going to hold a large dance, inviting British and German soldiers and civilians. He said it'll be a Peace Dance!" Agatha's sentence leaves everyone anxious, focusing on what she'd said.

"Agatha, don't toy with my feelings. Is that true?" asks Tina, who'd stopped eating.

"There, Agatha. You and your stories! Imagine. Germans and British soldiers together? Now?" Sarah questions.

"I don't know if it's true or not, but I heard my father talking, and he wouldn't joke around with his soldiers like that!" Agatha exclaims, now rather agitated.

Everyone at the table begins talking loudly and laughing impatiently, except for the girl who's still thinking about everything her father had told her.

"Jane, do you mean not even a dance will cheer you up?" Debby asks, looking at Jane, who seemed to be on another planet.

"I'm sorry, I wasn't paying any attention to what you were saying." Jane wakes up from her thoughts.

"I don't know what you were thinking about, but I'm giving you something better," Agatha says. "I heard my father say we're going to have a dance here on the base, understand? A dance!" Agatha exclaims, ecstatic, shaking Jane's hand.

"A dance?" Jane inquires, feeling a slight tremor inside.

"Yes, silly, a dance!" responds Debby, already rather excited.

"But is it a dance for young people? Or will our parents go, too?" Jane asks, getting up from the table, rather upset.

"I'm hoping that, if we're lucky, it won't be with our parents," Tina says.

"My father would certainly spoil everything," complains Agatha, crossing her arms.

"Could it really be true?" queries Jane, with her hands on her head.

"Jane, why are you so worried? Haven't you ever been to a dance without your parents," Sarah asks, somewhat concerned with Jane's despair.

"Without my parents?... No, never," Jane stammers, returning slowly to her chair.

"I'll bet she's never even danced with a man," suggests Agatha, smirking.

Sarah notices Agatha's malice and Jane's despair. Rising from her seat, she sits back down next to Jane.

"Don't worry about that cobra, Agatha. If she bites her tongue, she'll die from her own venom," Sarah says, affectionately playing with Jane's hair.

"We'll all go together and, if you've never danced with a boy before, you'll be in luck, because you'll dance with a soldier, which is better than just any old boy," Tina insists, helping Sarah comfort Jane.

Debby then decides to join Sarah and Tina, which makes Agatha visibly angry. She'd always been the group's favorite.

"I'm not hungry!" Agatha alleges, leaving the room.

When Agatha stalks out, Sarah sticks her tongue out, pointing at the door, provoking much collective laughter.

# Chapter V

Jane leaves the room, thanking everyone for their support. Just before departing, she hears Sarah say that everyone should stick together. That way, they'd be able protect each other and nothing bad would happen to Jane.

She hears Sarah but enters a deep trance in which she doesn't even remember how she got to her room.

"A dance? Now? What would father say? Maybe I shouldn't go. And if I don't? Will the other girls pick on me?"

She had so many doubts that she lies down on her bed and begins to cry.

Over her reclusive 18 years, Jane had never suffered an emotional overload and this day's events had genuinely disturbed her.

Jane falls into a deep sleep from crying so much.

Margaret hears about the dance during the afternoon. As soon as her husband returns for dinner, she interrogates him.

"John, dear, is it true what they're saying about that Peace Dance? All of the mothers on the base are in a complete uproar, and the girls..." Margaret says, grasping her husband's arm.

"Yes, it is, dear. It's already being talked about? This was Sergeant Matt's idea. He says his soldiers need a distraction," John responds, removing his uniform.

"Yes, but …. Will German soldiers be invited, too?" Margaret inquires, distressed.

"We're negotiating peace, dear, not war. I spent the afternoon studying peace proposals with a German colonel. The idea of a dance was very well received by everyone," John responds, taking off his socks.

"I'll not let my daughter go to this immoral dance by herself!" Margaret exclaims, shouting.

Immediately after his wife yells, John stands up and puts his hand over Margaret's mouth.

"Don't shout, dear. Where are your manners? Remember we're not in this house alone," John says, removing his hand from his wife's mouth. "I will also not let my daughter go to that dance by herself," John continues.

"Thank God! Somebody with some common sense," Margaret asserts.

"She'll be there with the other young women from the base; she won't be alone," John comments, turning his back on his wife.

"What?" Margaret again shouts but lowers her tone when she sees her husband's expression. "My daughter with those girls we don't even know? Is that what you call company?" Margaret questions, making her husband turn around and look at her.

"Margaret, dear, Jane's 18 and has never been to a dance... I agree that we need to protect her, but I think we've turned our daughter into a shrinking violet. Watch Jane, look into her eyes, and you'll realize society confuses her. She doesn't know what to do," John asserts.

"That's true. She doesn't even know how to dress herself, and that's my fault," Margaret says, covering her face with her hands and sitting on the bed.

"It's our fault, dear. I've always helped you with the decisions about how to rear Jane and, if you've failed, so have I," John responds, sitting next to Margaret.

They both look at each other in silence.

"Dear, I think England and Germany will soon be going to war. When this happens, the spark of happiness will go out all over Europe..." John makes a small pause and sighs. "The German colonel and I have talked a lot. He assures me the dance would be a link for peace between our nations, among the young who'll be our future and that's why they should at least socialize while we're at peace, until further orders," John finishes up.

"But will the German colonel's entire base go?" Margaret questions.

"There are five girls here in this house, but there's more housing for sergeants and lieutenants on this base and on the German base as well," John responds, smiling. "Don't worry, there will be enough girls for those soldiers."

"Jane will never agree to go to that dance..." Margaret says, helping her husband dress.

"I know, which is why we should be strong and not give in to her. Jane needs to go to this dance for her own good." John makes a slight pause, sighs, and finishes. "I'm afraid Jane doesn't know how to live without us and her books. I think about that all the time."

Margaret lowers her head and nods approvingly to her husband.

# Chapter VI

Margaret proceeds to the dining room with her husband and looks for her daughter. When she sees everyone there except Jane, Margaret looks at her husband, motioning to him that she'd go look for her.

Opening the door of the girl's room, Margaret finds Jane sleeping on her bed, surrounded by books.

The scene terrifies Margaret. She realizes what her husband had said was true.

"Jane, Jane, Jane," Margaret repeats, delicately shaking her child.

"Mum, let me sleep. I'm tired," Jane answers, avoiding her mother's eyes.

"Tired from what?" I didn't see you all afternoon. You spent the whole time stuck in here," Margaret says, picking up the books on Jane's bed.

"I went out this morning and got tired. It was a long walk, Mum. I want to sleep," Jane explains, pulling a pillow over her head.

"Jane Myer, you will get up this minute. You'll get dressed and I'll wait for you downstairs. If you don't come, I'll be back up here with your father. Do you understand?" Margaret says all of this very nervous. Jane had never before heard her mother talk to her like that.

"Yes, ma'am. I'll come down," Jane answers.

Margaret slams Jane's door shut. After her mother leaves, she thinks, "First, my father yells at me, and now my mother... Am I doing something wrong here?" Thinking about this, Jane begins to cry again.

Fifteen minutes had gone by and Jane still hadn't shown up. Margaret was going to call her husband when she heard Jane.

"There's no need, Mum. I'm here," Jane says, showing her mother that she was wearing her new dress.

Margaret is pleased at seeing her daughter, but, compared to the other girls, Jane doesn't have adequate clothes.

"Tomorrow, you and I are going shopping," Margaret whispers in Jane's ear.

Jane knew her clothes looked nothing like what the other girls wore, but she was comfortable with them and felt a little sad, hearing her mother say that.

When they entered the dining room, everyone was talking. The table went silent as soon as Jane came in.

"Come here, child. I've saved you a seat next to your friends," John says to Jane, breaking the silence.

When Jane arrives, everyone was already being served the main course. A waiter asks if she wants the first course, but, feeling very embarrassed, she prefers to continue right along with the others.

"Have you asked your father yet, Agatha?" Tina inquires softly.

"I haven't been able to talk to him, but my mother told me he and Jane's father spent the afternoon with a German colonel," Agatha responded, whispering.

Everyone looked at Jane.

"I haven't talked to him yet, if that's what you want to know," Jane calmly states.

Sarah asks where Jane had been, before adding, "We spent the afternoon looking at magazines and choosing dresses for the dance. What did you do?"

"I was tired. I read a little and fell asleep" Jane answered.

"The trip here from England really is very tiring," Debby helps out, winking at Jane.

"My father won't ever tell me about the dance. We'll only find out when they put the posters up," Agatha says impatiently, looking at Jane.

"I'll ask Dad after supper," Jane proposes, with all eyes on her.

Jane didn't believe there'd be a dance, since her last conversation with her father showed no hint of a celebration.

But, whatever, she needed to know so she could put the matter at hand to rest once and for all.

"Hooray for Jane!" Agatha loudly exclaims.

Everyone shouts, happy and excited, except for Jane, who remains emotionless.

John observes his daughter from a distance and realizes how unhappy she is. His heart as a father aches, but he knew he needed to do something.

After dinner, the men go to the veranda to smoke cigars, the women sit in the dining room for tea, and the girls run to the library, pulling Jane along with them.

John observes his daughter's total indisposition in joining the group and decides to act.

"Good evening, girls! May I steal my daughter for just a bit?" John asks the girls, good-naturedly.

"Of course, colonel," Agatha responds, winking at Jane and pushing her toward her father.

She felt increasingly dreadful; she knew that her father had noticed her sadness. "He always does," she thought. Jane knew her father would try to find out why, but she didn't want him to worry about her. After all, a war was looming.

"Yes, Dad, what do you want talk with me about?" Jane asks, forcing a smile.

John leads her to a garden. When both are alone, he takes Jane's hand.

"Pumpkin, I know you're sad. You don't have to pretend, mainly because you're terrible at it," John states, smiling.

Jane smiles a little, but tears stream from her eyes.

"I know you feel lost, that everything's new and confusing, and you certainly miss our home," John says, drying his daughter's tears with a handkerchief.

Jane shakes her head, confirming what her father'd said.

"Try to understand, dear. The world is here, outside your books, not in them," John says, showing Jane the garden.

"I know that, Dad. I like this world; I like it a lot," Jane responds, also pointing at the garden. "It's that world that makes me sad," Jane contends, pointing at the house.

"What's wrong with that world, darling?" her father inquires.

"Everything, Dad! Everything!" Jane exclaims, crying. "The people are futile, superficial. They're more worried about this…" Jane points to her dress, "… than this!" She now points at her heart.

"But how can you judge your friends like that? You've only known them for a day," John probes.

"I know, Dad. I've watched them, I've listened to them. You weren't there," Jane says, lowering her head.

"Jane, I'm sure none of those young women is more intelligent or more beautiful than you, but none of them deserves your prejudice, after so short a time," John explains, once again holding his daughter's hand. "Wars most often start because of some baseless prejudice. Both sides use physical force to reach a conclusion, which probably could have been arrived at if no one had pre-judged anything."

Jane wipes the tears from her face.

"I'm not being prejudiced, Dad!" she responds, offended.

"Then don't act prejudicially," John affirms, looking into his daughter's eyes.

"I think you're right, father. I should give these girls a chance, don't you think?" Jane says, a little more cheerfully.

"That's the Jane that I've reared and love so much, my brave little soldier. Fight this battle with your head held high. Always remember this," John recommends, kissing Jane's forehead.

It had been a while since John had called Jane "little soldier". He'd always called her that when she was little. "Don't let go of the handlebars. Stick with it, little soldier!" Jane remembers when her father kisses her.

John was going back to the house when Jane remembered the promise she'd made the girls.

"Dad, can I ask you something before you go back inside?" Jane askes.

"Yes, dear. What is it?"

"The girls heard that we're going to have a dance soon and that you and Agatha's father were discussing it this afternoon," Jane paused briefly. "I don't imagine it's true, but I wanted to hear it from you."

"Well, first, let me make it clear that your father is the worst person on earth to discuss social events like dances with. Second, I'm on a diplomatic mission and every afternoon, I'll discuss something with someone..." John paused again, as he perceived his daughter's anxiety about hearing his answer. "And, in the third place..." John paused again upon realizing his daughter's real interest, "a young lady like you shouldn't be paying attention to gossip," John continued, smiling.

"I know, Dad, but it's that the girls..." and before Jane could finish her sentence, John continued.

"And, fourth, young lady, yes, we'll soon be having a dance," John informed her, smiling.

"So, it's true, father? The soldiers really have been invited? Will you and Mum go? What day will it be?" Jane entered a deep state of anxiety and her father, fearing that she'd faint, embraced his daughter and said, "Yes, it's true, darling. The soldiers will go. However, your mother and I will go to a separate dance and, no, I don't know what day it'll be... Phew! Have I quelled your doubts?" John asks, smiling, releasing his daughter from his grip.

"My, the girls will pass out when I tell them the news!" Jane exclaims, excited about it for the first time.

"Jane, don't gossip. Limit yourself only to answering their questions, understood?" John orients her. She replies with a thumbs up.

Jane returns to the house and senses that her conversation with her father has had an effect. In fact, she even felt a spark of happiness in her heart.

As soon as Jane opens the library door, the girls calm down and watch in agony as Jane takes a seat on the sofa near the fireplace.

Agatha seemed to be the most anxious of the group at that moment, so Jane felt a bit of pleasure in saying nothing, watching Agatha's agony.

"I can't stand the suspense. Spit it out, Jane! Did you ask you father?" Agatha questions, agitated.

"Yes, I spoke with him," Jane responds, leafing through a magazine and forcing herself not to break out laughing.

"So, what did he say?" Agatha asks.

"Come on, Jane, that girl's practically having a stroke!" Debby exclaims, grinning.

Jane smiles for a few seconds, since she finds Agatha's despair about something she considers valueless to be amusing.

"Yes, Agatha, my father said there will be a dance. Feel better now?" Jane asks.

All the girls explode with joy from what Jane says and Agatha stands up, the most excited of them all.

"My, then it's true... I knew it... the soldiers will go!... Will my mother go? Will your father go? Where will the dance be? When is it? What type of dress should I wear? I need to talk to my mother. I don't have any clothes! Will my father let me go?" Agatha stops talking for a few seconds because she's out of breath.

The other girls start laughing at Agatha's despair. Jane stands up, puts her magazine away, and walks to the door of the library.

"Agatha, the only thing I know is that there will be a dance and the soldiers will go..." Jane quickly pauses, trying to remember her father's responses. "My father says the dance is for young people, so our parents won't be going."

Finishing the sentence, Jane turns to leave the library, but Debby runs to stop her.

"Jane, where are you going? We need to start thinking about our dresses, shoes, hair. The quicker we start, the better the results," Debby suggests, supported by the group.

"I don't like dances very much. I probably won't go. All of you can have fun for me," Jane says. She avoids listening to the girls' responses, protesting her position on the matter.

Jane returns to her room, lies down on her bed and thinks, "Imagine, me at this dance? I don't really care to be part of such futility." Jane begins to put her pajamas on and remembers her conversation with her father. "I promised Dad I'd try, but I didn't promise I'd go to a dance."

Jane then lies down and quickly falls asleep.

# Chapter VII

Getting up, Jane checks her clock and sees that she's managed to awaken on time. She dresses quickly and goes downstairs for breakfast.

Entering the dining room, she sees the tables already set and the staff finishing up with their food service.

"I got here on time today!" Jane exclaims to one of the waiters, who smiles and pours her a bit of tea.

Minutes later, Jane's parents enter the dining room accompanied by another two couples. Seeing that Jane was already at the table, John smiles and winks at her. She notices her father's satisfaction and smiles because she's finally gotten something right there.

Breakfast goes smoothly that morning and even Jane's new friends manage to stay quiet.

After eating, the officers take leave of their families for another day of negotiations. Jane, nevertheless, hugs her father very affectionately and whispers in his ear, "Dad, you don't need to worry about me. I'm going to be sociable, but I've decided not to go to the dance, no matter when it's held. I've got no desire to participate in any social event here. I think it's disrespectful to celebrate at a time like this."

Hearing what Jane said, John's features changes from happiness to deception, which she immediately notices and, thus, avoids meeting her father's eyes.

"Dear, we'll talk about this later, in case you don't change your mind."

John leaves his daughter and approaches Margaret. Jane notices her father whispering something to her mother, whose face also moves from joy to irritation.

The officers retire, and the women gather in the gazebo to talk. Jane avoids looking at her mother or anyone else; she prefers observing the details of the Alps, close to the base, and the flowers in the garden. Without realizing it, Jane has isolated herself from the group and walks rather happily through the garden, when she's surprised by her mother.

"I think you know what I've come here to talk about," Margaret asserts, taking her daughter's hand and walking through the garden, away from the gazebo, where everyone else watches attentively.

"Jane's such a fool!" Agatha exclaims, seated beside her mother in the gazebo.

"Behave, girl!" Agatha's mother reprimands, pinching her discretely.

"Stop, Mum! That hurts!" Agatha complains, moving her mother's hand. "But she really is, Mum!" Agatha insists. "Can you believe she doesn't want to go to the dance?"

Agatha covers her mouth with her hand, realizing she's said too much.

All the girls shoot Agatha a dirty look.

"I've already said it!" Agatha exclaims.

All the women look at Agatha's mother, who covers her face with her hand and says, "My daughter's mouth is bigger than her ears!"

She pauses for a moment, looks at her daughter, and continues, "Okay. Go ahead and finish what you started!"

Agatha seems relieved by her mother's order and repeats, with details, everything she heard Jane say the night before.

"Mum, I don't belong here!" Jane confirms, weeping.

"Dear, you belong anywhere you want. You're young, beautiful, and very intelligent..." Margaret stops briefly before going on. "Your problem, for which your father and I feel responsible, is that you can't and don't know how to socialize." It's now Margaret whose eyes are filled with tears.

"No, Mum. That's not it!" Jane responds, pulling herself together and embracing her mother. "You and Dad are excellent parents and I do know how to socialize, but these girls ... Mum, these girls are so vulgar!" Jane explains.

"Jane Myer, that is not how I reared you to be! You may be a wallflower, but you've never been a loose-tongued gossip!" says Margaret, irritated.

"It's not gossips, Mum. It's true!" Jane exclaims, raising her voice.

"My child, we haven't even been here a week. How can you have reached such a precise conclusion about your friends' vulgarity? That's gossip and speculation from a young lady who's afraid to socialize."

"No, it's not, Mum!" Jane sits down on a bench in the garden, covers her face with her hands, and begins to cry.

Margaret feels even more guilty for having kept her daughter secluded all these years. She sits down next to Jane and puts her daughter's head in her lap.

"Jane, it really hurts to see you suffering this way because of my mistakes. I'm afraid you don't know how to live without me and your father. I fear for your future, so I'll fight for your present," Margaret justifies, caressing Jane's hair.

"Mum, I never wanted to make you and Dad cry," Jane says, drying her tears and sitting up from her mother's lap.

"We're not crying because of you, but because of what we've done wrong," Margaret responds.

"I don't see any error in my upbringing, Mum. I'm crying because I want to keep it that way," Jane finishes up.

"These girls belong to the British elite. Like you, they're the daughters of our country's best military leaders, and I don't believe those young women have had an upbringing different from yours," Margaret states.

"But they're different, I guarantee. Look at their clothes, their shoes, the way they talk. They're nothing like me," responds Jane, pointing at her garments.

"That's another of my mistakes, my child," Margaret says, lowering her head. "You don't know how to dress like the princess you are… and I'm going to fix that."

"Mum, I'm not like those girls. I don't like short dresses, low necklines, or rouge," Jane asserts, upset.

"Jane, such modesty for a young woman of your age! It sounds like something my mother'd say, not my daughter," Margaret smiles at Jane.

"Grandmother was married to the same man for 56 years and I never noticed any problem in their relationship, so it makes me proud to think like her," Jane responds.

"Jane, there was rouge when I met your father, and all the girls were using it, including me. Do you think I'm vulgar? Do you think my relationship with your father is worse than your grandmother's?" Margaret questions.

Jane just shakes her head no.

"So, my child, learn something from your old mum who loves you very much. It's not the clothes or the makeup that defines character. It's your attitude."

Margaret stands up and takes Jane's hand. "If you're right and those girls are vulgar, the world will teach them a lesson. I can guarantee that, but it won't be my daughter who judges them, okay?"

Once again, Jane shakes her head yes.

"So, my dear, Princess Jane Myer's going to lift her head, accept her mother's advice, face the world dressed like a princess, and be respected like a queen."

Jane smiles, stands up from the bench and responds firmly, "Yes, Mum. I'll try."

Both of them return to the gazebo, where the main topic was preparations for the dance.

Upon entering the gazebo, Jane realizes all eyes are on her, which makes her blush.

"Well, well. I see the news about the dance is now in the public domain," Margaret smiles, pointing at her daughter, who sits at her side.

Everyone beings to smile and preparations for the dance continue.

# Chapter VIII

After having been at base for a month, Jane is a little more familiar with makeup and new dresses, even though high heels are still a challenge.

"That dress would be perfect with these heels, sweetheart," Margaret points out.

"But Mum, I can't walk in them! These shoes were made to torture whoever puts them on," Jane points out, laughing.

Every morning that month, Jane spent time with her new friends, who limit themselves to places where there were troops. What first seemed like torture was now routine, but she still hadn't talked to any soldiers. It was always the same story; she'd sit underneath her welcoming tree with a good book while her companions showed the soldiers all of their charms.

At first, Jane's attitude seemed strange but as the days passed by and she ceased being the group's focus of attention; they'd gotten used to her unique traits.

Returning home, Agatha sees a poster pasted on the wall.

"Peace Dance – Germany and England in a unique and pacific encounter of both nations!"

"Oh my! The dance is in two weeks! Now it's official! Look, girls," Agatha points out, excited.

"Holy Kamoly! I thought they'd given up on it!" Sarah exclaimed.

"They hadn't. They just hadn't found a place easily accessible to both bases," Jane responded, almost emotionlessly.

"And now, have you given up on all that silly talk about not going to the dance?" Debby asks.

Everyone looks at Jane, waiting for an answer.

"Apparently, my parents think that, if I don't go to this dance, my social life will end, and I'll be condemned to spend the rest of my days crying and unhappy, since I won't know how to live without them… The connection between those two arguments seems overstated to me, but…" Jane doesn't finish her sentence. She just shrugs, ironizing her argument.

"Does that mean you're going?" Agatha asks.

"For the good of British civilization, I am pleased to inform the public that Jane Myer will, indeed, attend the Peace Dance," Jane declares ironically, smiling as she enters the house.

"Don't worry, Jane, we'll all be together. I'm going to ask my mother to bring us some dresses from London!" Sarah exclaims.

Everyone is smiling and excited, except for one young lady who is indifferent.

"Great. I've always dreamed of putting on a dress from London," Jane continues, still ironic, before realizing that none of them understands irony. She just smiles to herself.

The week passes quickly and, finally, the dresses arrive at the mansion.

"Look, Mum, everybody, our dresses!" Agatha screams.

"Come on, dear, show a little excitement! I'm sure none of them will be as pretty as you!" Margaret encourages her.

Jane, in her habitual state of mind about clothes and shoes, drags herself to where the clothes are.

Everyone stands up excitedly, bouncing and twirling in their dresses. Jane merely comments that her dress was tight and came only to her knees, which makes her uncomfortable.

"My God, Mum! I can barely breathe in this! And the skirt? It's going to be cold!" Jane complains.

Jane's dress was blue, which matched her eyes. Imported lace covers her bust and part of her knees, but it was slightly translucent, which made her even more uncomfortable.

"Pumpkin, you look beautiful in blue. It makes your eyes stand out!" Margaret exclaims, ignoring Jane's habitual complaints.

"Mum, I can't breathe!" Jane reinforces.

Margaret checks Jane's waist and realizes her daughter is just exaggerating.

"When I was young, dresses were even tighter in the waist and I didn't die. You're lovely!" Margaret compliments her.

"All right, then, but… and the cold?" Jane asks.

"It shows you've never been to a dance, my child…" Margaret says, smiling. "… with all the dancing and those handsome men, the last thing you'll feel is cold," Margaret smiles at Jane, who doesn't seem to find any humor in what her mother's saying.

"And that's the only reason you're insisting on my going, right? Because you want me to find a man, marry him, and leave you," Jane says, sadly.

"The last thing your father and I want is to see you far away and the first thing we desire is for you to be happy!" Margaret justifies.

"I was happy in England. Here, I'm just a dressed-up, brainless doll," Jane insisters, rather hostilely.

"And, you'll soon be a toothless one, if you keep on behaving like this," Margaret suggests, annoyed.

"I'm sorry, Mum, I didn't mean to be disrespectful," Jane responds.

"Cheer up, honey, we're sending you to a dance, not a prison," Margaret says before leaving the room to find shoes that match the dress.

Seeing that she's alone, Jane decides to look in the mirror. She realizes, for the first time, that she's pretty and how perfectly the dress fits her.

"Okay! The dress is gorgeous, but I'd still rather be in a prison with it, than go to a dance with them." Jane grasps how ridiculous her comparison is and begins to laugh to herself.

"I see that my young lady realizes how lovely she is!" her mother exclaims, smiling, putting a pair of shoes on the floor.

"Try these on!" Margaret commands, pointing at them.

Janes slips the shoes on and almost falls because she doesn't know how to walk in heels.

"Listen, Mum. Do you expect me to dance with these or just try to stay on my feet all night? I'm not wearing these," Jane says.

"We'll talk about this later," Margaret smiles, awed by her daughter's beauty.

# Chapter IX

The most anxiously awaited day of the year finally arrives for Agatha, Tina, Debby, and Sarah. Jane, in turn, seems to look at it as if it were just one more day out of many.

Margaret, however, was rather happy and excited.

Because it was a Saturday, John doesn't go to work and decides to help Margaret in the difficult struggle to convince their daughter to cheer up for the event.

"Come on, sweetheart, it's not that difficult. When you least expect it, you'll be enjoying yourself like you've never done before!" John encourages her, bouncing his daughter on the bed.

"Dad, I want to make it clear that I'm doing this because I love you very much," Jane says, getting up off the bed. "I don't understand how a dance can have as much effect on my life as you think," Jane finished, going to the bathroom in her suite.

"Dear, it's not the dance that will change you, but getting to know a new world," Margaret explains.

"What world?" Jane queries.

"A world that only you can discover. You can be sure we'll be with you. Even if that world seems frightening to you, remember us," John responds, with tears in his eyes.

Jane doesn't pay much attention to her parents. For her, it's all just a worried father exaggerating.

John, in turn, waits for Jane to enter the bathroom and begins to weep.

"Don't over react, dear!" Margaret tells her husband.

"I know, honey, but it's the first time I actually realize my daughter's growing up and is needing me less," John explains, drying his tears.

"She isn't getting married, John. She's only going to a dance. Like father, like daughter!" Margaret exclaims, smoothing Jane's dress on the bed.

Leaving the bathroom, Jane notices that her mother's getting her dress ready and separating her makeup, among other preparations.

"Mum, it's eight o'clock in the morning. The dance is in the evening. What are you doing?" Jane asks.

"I'm doing what the other mothers are also doing. I'm helping get things ready," Margaret responds, continuing with what she was doing.

"That's mad, Mum! I'm going down for breakfast! And, I'll bet no one else is getting ready yet," Jane communicates, leaving her mother in her room.

Reaching the dining room, Jane's surprised to find only men eating breakfast.

"Sweet pea, the waiter's taking your and your mother's breakfast to the room. You didn't need to come down," John says to her, escorting Jane to the main staircase.

"Dad, it's eight o'clock. You don't mean it'll take eleven hours for me to get ready, do you?" Jane asks.

"Daughter… I don't understand women's things, but your mother told me you were running late," John answers, making her go back to her room.

Jane reaches the room and surrenders to her mother's desires without questioning or getting in her way.

Nine hours later, she's almost ready.

"What do you mean, I'm almost ready? My God! This is the longest day of my life!" Jane exclaims, extremely tired and bored.

"Calm down, dear, your hair is long and it's hard to fix," Margaret responds, inspecting the hairdresser's every movement as she helps Jane out.

She could only think about how tired she already was, and the night hadn't begun yet. Her head was filled with a mixture of anxiety, indifference, and happiness. At that point, it was difficult to define any one of those sensations more deeply.

After endless hours of primping, the girls were ready.

"My God, Jane! You're beautiful!" Agatha lauded her.

"We all are," Jane responded.

John was excited and happy seeing his daughter looking like a real princess.

"Have fun, sweetheart!" John says, kissing her forehead." You're the most beautiful princess in the world!"

Jane smiles and thanks her father for his affectionate words.

"Daughter, remember, try to keep the weight of your body on your tiptoes and force your calves..." She pauses and kisses Jane. "You're lovely! No one is as beautiful as you, my pumpkin!" Margaret says proudly, next to Jane's ear.

Jane then leaves the mansion with her friends, who can't manage to stop smiling and dancing.

She continues walking with the girls until her parents are no longer in view.

"Are we walking to the dance?" Jane asks.

"I thought that's horrible, too, Jane, but my father said it'd seem aggressive if we arrive at the dance in an English car," Tina responds.

Jane takes hold of one of Tina's arms.

"Stop for a minute, girls. I need to take my shoes off!" Jane exclaims, irritated. "Force my calves... I'm going to lose my toes, that's what!" she complains, removing her shoes.

"Jane, are you crazy? It's a kilometer to the dance and your stockings will be filthy!" Agatha says, pointing at the muddy ground.

"You're the ones who are crazy. I like my feet!" Jane exclaims again, smiling because she's barefooted.

# Chapter X

After walking a kilometer, the girls reach the entrance to the dance and hear the music inside.

"We're late!" Agatha exclaims, beginning to run.

Sarah grabs her friend's arm, keeping her from continuing.

"Calm down, Agatha. Patience… we've waited until now and we can wait a bit longer," says Sarah, who walks slowly to the entrance.

They were already at the door, when Debby shouts, "Wait, girls. We walked a lot. We should touch up our makeup."

At that point, they all pulled makeup and mirrors out of their purses. Jane, on the other hand, found a spot to support herself and put her shoes back on. Realizing that her stockings were a little muddy, she decides to take them off and wear her shoes without them.

"Jane, you're a little sweaty. It might be better for you to put on some face powder," Debby advises, offering some to Jane.

"No, thanks. I'm already looking like a clown and the air will dry the sweat off, since we're freezing out here," Jane says, shivering a little.

"Cold? It's not cold at all!" Agatha insists, smiling, looking at the entrance to the dance.

"You pulled your stockings off. That's why you're cold!" Sarah justifies.

"Simmer down, Agatha. The night's young!" Tina responds, looking for something in her purse. "Since we're far from the base, I think this will help us get in the mood for the dance!" She finishes, pulling a pack of cigarettes from her purse.

Everyone smiles and takes one. Jane just looks at the cigarettes and the girls. A few weeks ago, their attitude about smoking would have startled her, but after everything she's seen in that group, nothing surprises Jane.

"Don't you want a cigarette to relax, Jane?" Sarah asks.

"No, thanks. I have other ways to relax," Jane replies, pulling a book from her purse.

At that moment, all the girls chuckle about Jane's attitude, which doesn't bother her at all.

Near the entrance to the dance, a Kubelwagen, a German all-purpose vehicle, approaches with five duly uniformed soldiers, all smiling and smoking.

"So, Heinz? It's going to be a good night, don't you think?" one of the soldiers asks the driver, in German.

Heinz was the oldest in the group and, also, the handsomest and most athletic. He was known by his colleagues as a lady's man. And he was always surrounded by girls who sometimes took turns going out with the athletic, tall, blond-haired, green-eyed Heinz.

The soldiers were proud of just being in the vehicle with Heinz, since they had no doubt about his ability to find girls not only for himself, but for the entire group.

"Our objective is to interact with the English, and I have a lot of English to interact with the girls if you know what I mean," responds Heinz, smiling and parking the transport near the entrance.

"Look, girls, German soldiers!" Agatha exclaims, looking at them.

"Agatha, pipe down! Remember to flirt first," Debby says, smiling and looking at the young men.

Everyone imitates Debby, except for Jane, who merely raises her eyes to look at the Kubelwagen. She then covers face back up with her book and starts reading again.

Meanwhile, in the vehicle, the soldiers finish smoking their cigarettes, exchanging glances and smiles with the girls.

"Well, boys..." Heinz pauses, throwing his cigarette butt out, "it's time to practice our English!"

They jump out of the car, while Heinz signals them to stop.

"What is it, Heinz? Isn't it time to practice our English?" one of them says, speaking into Heinz's ear.

"Gentlemen! Divide and conquer," Heinz responds, smiling. "You can't go attack them all at once.

You have to have an objective, make them feel special... 'I'm yours', understood?" he asks them, grinning.

They all smile and agree with his strategy and begin discussing who will go after whom.

"Wait, everyone, I think our boss has the right to choose first!" one of the soldiers exclaims.

"Heinz, do you want that blonde?" referring to Agatha, the one who was most obviously looking at them.

"She'll be easy and, if the prey is easy, there's no thrill in the chase," he responds, smiling. "I'll leave her for you, since you're the youngest," Heinz finishes up.

They all smile and joke with the soldier.

"I prefer more interesting and more difficult prey," Heinz pause, before continuing. "I'll take that shy one over there, off to the side."

"That one with the book?" asks one of the soldiers. "I can't even see her face!" he finishes.

"What about the face? I can see the rest, and the rest is perfect and more useful," Heinz responds, smiling.

"I don't know, Heinz. She hasn't even looked at us. I think she'll spend the night reading," one of the soldiers stresses.

"I'll bet one hundred marks that, by the end of the night, she'll be mine!" Heinz bets, turning to the soldier who spoke last.

The soldier shakes Heinz's hand, the group gets out of the vehicle and walks toward the girls.

"Oh, my God! They're coming over here," Agatha says, excited, fixing her hair." Their uniforms are so pretty!" she exclaims.

At that moment, Jane, as always, dives deeper into her book and thinks, "It's going to start now…"

The young men approached and began courting their respective girls, in English.

"Oh, my! Your English is perfect!" Tina exclaims.

The soldier with her responds, smiling, "Just our English?"

Everyone chuckles and takes their soldiers' arms. Jane remains motionless.

"Why don't you boys be courteous and accompany the English ladies to the dance?" Heinz suggest, pointing to the entrance.

The soldiers quickly understand Heinz's intentions and walk their girls to the dance, leaving him alone with Jane.

Jane, hearing her companions move away, becomes slightly desperate and decides not to lower the book from her face. "We were all going to stick together," Jane remembers in her thoughts. "Maybe, if I stay quiet, with the book covering my face, he'll go away, and I can go in later," Jane thinks.

A few minutes go by in complete silence. Heinz lights another cigarette and sits down next to her, which makes Jane feel extremely uncomfortable. The silence is beginning to really bother Jane and she decides to look quickly at Heinz, who notices her glance and begins to smile.

Heinz's smile makes Jane blush even more and she decides to break the silence.

"What did you think was so amusing?" Jane asks, irritated, without lowering the book.

Heinz smiles, pulls out a white handkerchief from his pocket and waves it, looking at Jane who, with the movement, looks at his hands and then at his green eyes, which immediately catch her attention.

"I think I'm at the wrong dance. This was supposed to be a 'Peace Dance', right?" Heinz comments, putting his hankie away.

Jane realizes that, in fact, Heinz was right and that the way she'd received him had been aggressive and unnecessary.

She then closes her book and looks at Heinz. Even if she tried, Jane wouldn't be unable to notice how handsome he was. For a few seconds, her hormones speak loudly, and she blushes.

"I think it warmed up a little, don't you?" Heinz asks, smiling, noticing her rosy glow.

"So, how much was the bet for?" Jane asks, recovering her color and facing his green eyes.

Heinz is surprised for an instant. He hadn't expected that question, much less Jane's intelligence. He remains quiet for a few seconds, looks at Jane's blue eyes and says, "What makes you think there's a bet?" Heinz asks, eyeing Jane.

"I'm with a group of much prettier and easier girls, so I don't think I'd freely be your first choice," Jane justifies, looking for her purse and beginning to put her book away.

"Are you reading *Don Juan*?" Heinz inquires, pointing at the book Janes was stowing.

"No, but I've had the pleasure of reading *Don Juan* in the past," Jane responds, briefly enticed by the conversation. "It's *Metamorphosis*," she adds, closing her purse.

"Franz Kafka? An excellent author!' Heinz confirms. "I've heard it said he was from a country called Germany. Have you ever heard of it?" he asks, smiling.

"That must be why I'm not enjoying the book," Jane remarks, smiling for the first time.

"When you finish the book, we can come back to this topic," Heinz suggests, also smiling.

"Okay, you've got my attention! Now, at least, be honest and tell me how much the bet was for," inquires Jane.

"If I do, will you grant me at least one dance?" he proposes, offering Jane his hand.

"Why a dance? Was that the bet?" Jane asks, looking at Heinz's hand.

"Well, well, now I'm beginning to perceive a certain interest in my bet. Do you want to split the proceeds?" Heinz asks, smiling.

"What would I do with German money? I don't even know how much a piece of bread costs in your currency. I just want to know how much I cost you," Jane asks, intrigued.

"But, if you don't know the value of our money, how are you going to measure how much you cost me?", Heinz queries.

"Tell me in bread, then!' Jane exclaims, smiling.

"I want to make it absolutely clear that I placed the bet before speaking with you…" Heinz pauses and lowers his head. "It's not a fair price, now that I've had the pleasure of speaking with you," Heinz adds, still offering Jane his hand.

"Okay, I accept the dance!" Jane responds, taking Heinz's hand. "but we're going to make it clear that I am accepting only because I'm a lousy dancer and your feet will pay a high price, that way, you can learn not to judge any other lady," Jane straightens her back up and raises her head like royalty. He just smiles at Jane's daring.

Entering the dance hall with Heinz, Jane soon realizes she's not the only young woman to notice his beauty. All of the girl's eyes were staring at Heinz. Jane then began to be immensely pleased to be at his side, making the other girls jealous.

On the dance floor, Jane easily spots her companions, all of them being entertained with long kisses from the German soldiers. When Jane realizes what is going one, she blushes again, but, this time, in embarrassment at being part of that group of girls.

Because Heinz was older and more experienced, he looks at Jane and then her companions, grasping the entire situation and Jane's distress.

"It was more or less fifty pieces of bread, and I consider myself to have lost the bet," Heinz says, turning Jane's face and making her look at him.

"Why did you lose it?" Jane asks, hypnotized by the young man's charm and sensitivity.

"Because I bet that I'd be leaving with a girl similar to them, but shy," Heinz responds, pointing to her colleagues.

"And…?" Jane ask, anxious to hear the answer.

"And… that … you're nothing like them, so I lost!" Heinz asserts, pulling Jane in to begin dancing.

"How do you know I'm different," Jane inquires, trying to keep her balance in her heels.

"Well, in the first place, I doubt your friends even know what a book is and, if they did, I doubt they'd read *Metamorphosis*. In the second place, it wouldn't have been difficult to get you to come into the dance with me. In the third place, you wouldn't be forcing yourself to dance in these shoes. It'd come naturally," Heinz says, smiling.

"I hate these shoes," Jane exclaims, looking at her feet.

Heinz smiles and continues dancing with Jane, who is now radiant after hearing his response.

As Jane had said, she didn't know how to dance and continually stepped on his feet with her high heels.

"I think I understand your hatred of those shoes. I'm beginning to feel something similar," Heinz commented, smiling.

Dancing with Heinz, Jane radiates happiness, forgetting all her problems and fears. He, too, is quite happy in her company.

"I love the color of your stockings… flesh tone, right?" Heinz asks, smiling, noting that Jane was the only one not wearing stockings in the hall.

"It's a shame my shoes aren't flesh tone as well. I'd be much more comfortable," Jane says, smiling.

"I agree… I think we'd both be more comfortable," Heinz agrees with a grin. "What's your name?"

Jane perceives her lack of manners and responds, a little embarrassed.

"Forgive me for not introducing myself already. I'm Jane Myer," she responds.

"I'm Heinz Fritz. Are you related to Col. John Myer?" Heinz asks.

"Yes, he's my father. Do you know him?" Jane asks, fearful she'd said to much.

"Everyone knows the brave and respected Col. Myer. Your father's an excellent soldier. Now that I know who he is, I fear for my life," he says, smiling.

"My father would never do anyone harm if he were well behaved and respected his daughter," Jane asserts, looking at him.

"There's no need to repeat that," Heinz says, bowing to Jane who awkwardly covers her face.

Jane feels even prouder of her father.

"My father, above all, is a fair and honest man," Jane adds.

Heinz nods yes with his head and begins dancing again.

Jane is beginning to understand the dance steps when Heinz invites her to get something to drink. She accepts his invitation and Heinz accompanies her to an empty table where he leaves her to get their drinks. Jane watches him from afar and realizes that Heinz is limping because his feet hurt. She feels guilty, but, nevertheless, smiles at the young man.

Spotting Jane alone at the table, Agatha runs over to sit next to her.

"I'll bet you're adoring the dance, right?" Agatha asks, looking at Heinz.

"Are you enjoying yourself, Agatha?" Jane asks, perceiving her malice.

"It's the best night in my life!" Agatha responds.

Jane doesn't appreciate Agatha's company at that moment, but her good manners prevent her from asking the girl to leave.

"You're lucky. That soldier is SO handsome. Be careful or I'll steal him," Agatha comments.

Jane is startled when she realizes that Agatha's drunk. She knows Agatha is the youngest in the group and that she shouldn't be drinking.

"Agatha, have you been drinking?" Jane asks, concerned.

"Just a couple of beers to loosen up," Agatha replies.

"Who got the beer for you?" Jane asked, already sure of the answer.

Before she could respond, Heinz and the soldier with Agatha arrive, each holding two glasses of beer.

"Here, dear," says the soldier, handing one of the glasses to Agatha.

Heinz puts both of his glasses on the table and offers one to Jane, who quickly refuses the offer.

"One can quickly see that you're not German," Heinz responds, smiling while grabbing Jane's glass of beer.

Jane stands up from the table and begins to leave, when Heinz gently takes her hand.

"I'm sorry. I didn't mean to offend you. I just thought you liked beer," Heinz says, looking at Jane and Agatha.

"Don't mind her. She's always annoying like that!" a very drunk Agatha exclaims.

"Do you want me to get you something else to drink?", Heinz asks.

Jane was about to answer when Agatha and the soldier begin to kiss in a very vulgar manner. She lowers her head, embarrassed, and leaves the table.

Heinz observes the entire situation, grabs his beers and runs after Jane.

"Please, slow down or I'm going to drop everything!" Heinz exclaims.

"I've already said I didn't want any beer. Do you want to get me drunk? Like your friends are doing with my friends?" Jane asks angrily.

"No, I …" Heinz pauses. "I really like beer and I thought you might too, that's all." He points out another empty table for Jane to sit down. "Take care of my beer and I'll bring you something non-alcoholic."

"Do you intend to drink all of the beer in the house?" Jane queries, not interested in sitting down.

"I intended on drinking one glass, but since you don't want yours, I'm going to drink two. Throwing beer away during wartime is a sin in Germany," Heinz pauses. "Actually, wasting beer any time is a sin," he finishes up, smiling and pulling out a chair for Jane.

She smiles at his joke and takes her seat. Heinz doesn't take long to return with a glass of juice.

"The bartender must think I'm effeminate," Heinz says with a grin, and sits next to her.

Jane smiles again, and thanks him for the juice, takes a sip, and lowers her head.

"What did I do now?" Heinz asks, trying to look Jane in the eyes.

"You didn't do anything. I'm just sick of all this?" Jane replies.

"Are you sick of me or of the dance?" Heinz asks, quaffing half his glass in one gulp.

"You haven't done anything yet," Jane pauses, looks at Heinz, and goes on. "And I won't let you do, either... I'm tired of living at the base, I'm tired of them." She points at Agatha. "And I'm tired of pretending to be somebody I'm not!" Jane exclaims with tears in her eyes.

"How long have you been at the base? What kind of things have you done with them?" Heinz asks.

"Are those questions for military or personal ends?" Jane wants to know, remembering that Heinz was in the German army.

"I didn't remember I was in the army," Heinz responds, having just finished his first glass.

"My! That was fast," Jane exclaims, startled. "You're going to get drunk like that."

"I was thirsty. Trust me. Two glasses of beer is nothing for a German. We call this breakfast in Munich, where I'm from," Heinz pauses, "but that's not what I asked."

"I've been at the base a little over a month, but I think they've been here longer. As for our activities ... well... they're what you're seeing now," Jane responds.

"It must be awfully lonely for you," Heinz says, holding Jane's hand.

A chill she'd never felt before runs down her spine. Her heart beats faster and she realizes she needs to calm down. She observes, in a glance, that Heinz had finished the second glass while she hadn't even drunk half of her juice.

"You drink really fast!" Jane exclaims, changing the topic.

"This uniform's very hot, I'm burning up," Heinz complains, pulling at his collar. "Why don't we go get a little fresh air?" Heinz asks.

Jane's a bit apprehensive with that request, which Heinz notes before adding, "We won't go far, just to the poor. If you prefer, we can stay close to the English soldiers near the entrance."

Jane felt safer with the proposal and accepted his invitation.

Once outside, Heinz lights another cigarette.

"You didn't answer about feeling lonely at the base," Heinz inquires again.

"I don't mind being alone. I actually prefer the company of a good book to that of a person who adds nothing," Jane says, leaning against a wall far from his cigarette.

"You don't smoke?" Heinz asks, noting Jane's distance.

"No, I'm a country girl. I prefer healthy living!" Jane responds.

"I have the opposite problem. I like to smoke, drink, and be in the company of other people," Heinz says, smiling.

"Do you feel lonely?" Jane asks, noticing that Heinz's expression changes.

"Sometimes it's lonelier being surrounded by people than when reading a book," Heinz replies, putting his cigarette out.

"I really understand what you're saying. I'll bet you suffer more than I do," Jane says, observing Heinz's face.

"We all wear masks. I'm older and have been using mine longer. That's the difference," Heinz asserts, leaning next to Jane.

"Why do we need masks? Why do we need to be someone different from who we are?" Jane asks.

"I don't know. I mean... I only know why I have to use a mask, not why you do," Heinz says.

"So maybe that's where we're different. You know why you need a mask, but I don't..." Jane replies.

"If I'm a good looking, healthy and intelligent young man, I don't get any respect. I need to be Heinz, the lady's man, the wiseman, the teacher... I don't understand what I teach, but I teach something," Heinz says, reflecting.

"Why do you think you won't get any respect from your group being handsome, intelligent, and kind, like you are with me?... You've got my respect. Maybe this way, you can get the same results with your friends," Jane asserts.

Heinz reflects about what Jane says and asks, "Why are you wearing those shoes you detest?", pointing at Jane's feet.

"I was forced to! Just like I was forced to put on this dress, pull my hair back, and paint myself like an Indian," Jane answers, exaggerating.

"You don't look like you're a child any longer. If you didn't want to, you wouldn't need to put any of that on," Heinz says.

"My parents think it's important," Jane responds.

"Do you think it's important?" Heinz asks. He receives a "no" as an answer. "So, if you don't think it's important, why don't you tell your parents?" Heinz continues.

"I tried talking with them, but they think I'm a wallflower, that I need this to socialize," Jane says.

"That's my point. I need this to socialize," Heinz pauses. "Sometimes we do things that we don't like in order to achieve a result."

"Why do you need to socialize by being a cheap lady's man?" Jane asks.

"Because it works the quickest! If I were to tell my soldiers to be respectful with women, they'd call me effeminate and no one would obey me. But, if I teach them to take women to bed, they'll risk their lives at my side." Heinz looks at Jane and perceives her startled face. "I wish I had more elaborate motives, but I don't."

"I'm sure you must be suffering, going out with all those girls," Jane says ironically.

"And I'm sure that you hate having men look at you in that dress," Heinz adds, smiling.

Jane starts to smile because she was feeling good about herself at that moment and understands what Heinz is trying to say.

"So, you think it's right to wear a mask? To deceive? To be someone I'm not?" Jane asks.

"I think you always need to be shrewd, always! You should analyze all situations and, if you think you need to dress like this on the base to make your parents happy, then do it and enjoy yourself while you're at it. Don't look at it like it's torture, or you'll be unhappy for the rest of your life," Heinz says.

"You mean I should wear these clothes and enjoy myself; you're a lady's man so you'll be respected, but you have fun. Is that it?" Jane queries.

"I do have a lot of fun," Heinz replies, smiling. "When I was a teenager, it was easy to date girls and I realized that the more I went out with them, the more they hated me and the more the boys respected me. I decided to use that until it got old, but now, in the army, it works the same way. In reality, it's even better, since I need them to trust me like I trust them. And if this is a way to get those results, why not?" Heinz finishes up.

"Are you those boys' superior?", Jane asks.

"Yes, I'm a sergeant, and that's part of my squad," Heinz responds.

"How old are you?" Jane asks.

"I'm 63. I know I'm well preserved," Heinz responds, screwing up his face.

"Then you're not much older than me. I'm 60," Jane asserts, going along with the joke.

"If you older than 20, I'm going to be impressed," Heinz says, turning Jane's face.

"I'm 18. And you?" Jane asks.

"I'm 23 and I knew you were still a child," Heinz says.

"You just offered me a beer and now I'm a child?" Jane argues.

"The first time my father gave me a beer, I was ten years old, and by the time I was 18, I'd drunk a lot of beer."

"At ten, I remember drinking fresh milk, almost straight from the cow," Jane comments.

"The English really are kind of queers," Heinz says, smiling while protecting himself from Jane, who playfully smacks him.

Their conversation continues intensely as they enjoy themselves, touching on things of mutual interest, like the books Jane's read or the trips Heinz has taken.

Jane became more and more interested in Heinz. She'd never talked with anyone who was interested in literature. Consequently, she found Heinz delightful.

Neither of them realized what time it was, nor did they notice anyone entering and leaving the dance. It was two in the morning when the British guard interrupted their conversation.

"It's late. Everyone should return to their bases," the soldier advised.

"My God, how time has flown!" Jane notes, realizing that the dance had ended, and she was alone with Heinz. "Where are my friends? I don't know how to get home without them!" Jane exclaimed, distressed, realizing that she'd been left alone in an unknown place in the middle of the night.

"If I take you to the British base, will you know how to get home?" Heinz asks, concerned.

Jane shakes her head yes and begins to cry. Heinz takes her hand and calms her.

"Don't worry. I don't want to harm you at all. I'll help you get home. I know the area well," Heinz replies.

The street was deserted when he opened the door of his vehicle for her.

"Get in. You can trust me."

Jane enters the Kubelwagen and they were on their way when Jane shouts, "Stop the car!"

"What is it, Jane?"

"This is a German transport. They might misunderstand when you enter the base," Jane says.

Heinz realizes that Jane's right. After all, it was only a "Peace Dance", but the threat of war still exists between the two countries.

Heinz then looks at Jane, takes her hand and replies. "You're right. I can't risk that, but I also can't leave you alone. My soldiers and I are camped not far from here. We can go there. I'll leave the vehicle and we can walk to the base," Heinz proposes.

Offering no resistance, Jane agrees with him and, arriving at the camp, the sound of loud music was in the air. Both exit the car.

"Jane, I need to change shoes. I can't walk in these. Some girl I danced with this evening left my feet swollen," Heinz jokes, making Jane smile.

He takes her hand and leads her inside the main tent. Upon entering, Jane sees clothes on the ground and hears shouting.

A little further in, she sees Agatha, Tina, Debby, and Sarah nude and having sex, shouting and enjoying themselves with the soldiers.

Jane glowers at Heinz, drops his hand, and runs out of the tent. Outside, she takes off her shoes and runs as fast as she can.

Heinz, desperate, chases after Jane, but because of his sore feet, it takes him a while to catch up to her and, as soon as he does, he forcefully grabs her arm and says, "I didn't know. I'm sorry!" Heinz exclaims.

Jane doesn't even let him finish his sentence when she jerks his hand from her arm.

"I knew it! That's what you wanted all along! And your conversation about masks… It was all a lie, just so you could get me here," Jane says, crying. "I'm just a bet for you, aren't I? You almost got what you wanted. You're disgusting!" Jane finishes, threatening to slap Heinz, but he restrains her hand.

"I've already said I consider it a lost bet; you aren't like them. I realized that immediately. I didn't know what was going on in there; I swear. I'd never hurt you! I wasn't disrespectful at any point with you and I thought I'd proven my good and real intentions with you!" Heinz releases Jane's hand and attempts to embrace her.

She lets him hug her but continues crying.

"I'm not like them. I'm not!" Jane keeps repeating, still crying.

Heinz takes a handkerchief from his pocket, dries a few of her tears and then hands it to her.

"I know that. You made that clear and proved it as well," Heinz affirms, releasing Jane, who begins to calm down. "Oh, my! Now your makeup's all runny. You look like a clown," he says, smiling, playing with Jane. "But you're the most beautiful clown I've ever met!" Heinz adds, kissing her forehead.

Jane calms down and Heinz sits on the ground.

"What are you doing?" Jane asks.

"If you can take your shoes off, so can I, right?" Heinz answers.

When he begins to remove his shoes, Jane immediately notices how read and swollen Heinz's feet are.

"Criminy! That girl you danced with is really bad, isn't she?" Jane says, now smiling.

"I think I'm going to survive," Heinz says.

They resume their trip to the British base. Their walk took a few minutes, during which Jane remained silent.

"I really didn't know. Don't you believe me?" Heinz queries.

"I do. If I didn't, you wouldn't be here. I'd have come alone," Jane responds crossly.

"Are you always this delicate when other people offer you help?" Heinz asks, not liking Jane's tone of voice.

"I'm sorry, I'm not upset with you, but with my great 'friends'", Jane explains, ironically.

"You don't need that type of friendship!" Heinz says.

"But that's the only kind I can have for now," she says sadly. "Should I tell anyone what I saw tonight?" Jane questions.

"It won't do you or them any good. Let life teach them," Heinz responds.

They were very close to the base when Heinz spots a British soldier approaching.

"Halt, soldier!" the British soldier exclaims.

Heinz immediately raises his hands.

"It's okay, soldier. I'm Jane Myer, Col. John Myer's daughter. We were at the Peace Dance and I got lost. This soldier was helping me."

The soldier lowers his rifle and motions for Jane to proceed. She had taken Heinz's hand and pulled him onto the base. However, the soldier once again raises his weapon and says, "Just her! You! Return to your base."

"Will you accompany her? It's late and dark," Heinz inquires, worried. "It's almost three in the morning. She's a young woman and shouldn't walk by herself."

"I can't leave my post," the soldier replies, a little confused.

Jane perceives the soldier's confusion and continues, "My father will have you brought up on charges if you make me go home alone. Let him go with me and, if he isn't back in fifteen minutes, sound the alarm and have him arrested," Jane suggests, with an authoritarian voice.

The soldier agrees with Jane and lets Heinz pass.

"Damn, I've stared my PT early today!" Heinz say, smiling while he runs.

"I hope you're paying attention, so you can get back. These soldiers are well trained and prompt," Jane advises, panting.

Running, Jane and Heinz reach the mansion in six minutes, a true record.

"You've got nine minutes to get back," Jane jokes.

Since she didn't want to have to explain what Heinz was doing there again, she decides to stop next to the mansion and say goodbye to him.

"Thanks for bringing me back. You've been a true gentleman," Jane says, clasping Heinz's hand.

"You're a lady and deserve it!" he replies, kissing her hand.

"It was a pleasure meeting you!" Jane adds, starting to walk toward the house.

"That's it?" Heinz asks anxiously.

"What do you mean? What do you expect?" Jane asks, looking at him.

"Tomorrow? I mean, today, later," Heinz says, smiling. "We're going on a picnic at the waterfalls. Have you been there?" Heinz asks.

Realizing that Jane hesitates before answering, Heinz continues, "We can go with your 'friends' and my 'friends'" Heinz ironizes. "I'll tell them when I get back. That way, you won't be alone with me. Do you accept?" Heinz asks, looking at his watch.

"Yes, I do! Now run or we'll never make it to that picnic together," Jane suggest, pointing in the direction of the base entrance for Heinz.

He throws her a kiss and runs.

Jane immediately goes into the mansion.

Everyone was sleeping, so she tries to make as little noise as possible. And, reaching her room, Jane is smiling broadly.

"Am I falling in love?" Jane asks herself.

Jane lies down in her bed and, for the first time at that base, she doesn't have to cry herself to sleep.

# Chapter XI

At six in the morning, Jane's parents stormed in her room. They seemed very worried.

"Good morning, Dad!" Jane exclaimed, even though she was very sleepy.

"Thank God you're here, Jane!" her father said, sitting down on her bed and putting his hand over his heart.

"Yes, Dad, I am! What happened? You seem very worried!" Jane replies, laying her head in her father's lap.

"What happened yesterday?" Margaret asks, vexed and hysterical.

Before Jane could answer, Margaret yells into the hall, "She's here!"

With Margaret's shouting, Jane's room is invaded by Agatha, Debby, Tina, and Sarah's desperate parents.

"Please, tell us what happened yesterday, Jane!" Agatha's father frantically asks, bathed in tears.

"We went to the dance…" Jane begins, rather embarrassed by the presence of so many people in her room.

"Yes, child, we know that. Begin by telling me how you got home," John questions, more relieved.

"I met a German soldier, we danced and talked all night." Jane pauses and then continues. "It got very late and I couldn't find the girls. Since I didn't know how to get home, the soldier brought me to the base..." Jane paused again. She wanted to tell what she'd seen in the German quarters but remembered Heinz's advice and finished up. "I came with him. If you don't believe me, you can ask the soldier on guard duty this morning. He let Heinz come in for just fifteen minutes. I ran really hard," Jane remembers, smiling.

"So, his name is Heinz?" Margaret inquires rather happily, holding Jane's hand.

John, nevertheless, is fairly worried, and Jane, observing her father's reaction, concludes, "Dad, he's a good young man. He was very respectful, and I didn't know how to get home..."

Jane is interrupted by her father, who asks her to be quiet.

"We're going to talk to the German army," John says. He's interrupted by Jane's scream.

"No, Dad! Please don't hurt him!" Jane exclaims, distraught, sorry that she'd given Heinz's name.

John, visibly irritated at having been interrupted, looks at Jane and says, "If Jane met a German soldier, perhaps your daughters did too, and they can help us with information about the last time they were seen," completes John, holding Jane's hand and looking at the other parents.

John's idea is well received by everyone and they leave her room. Her parents, in turn, stay close to Jane's bed.

"I'm very proud of you, daughter!" John affirms, kissing Jane's hand.

"I knew our Jane wouldn't let us down," Margaret says.

"What happened to the girls?" Jane asked, already suspecting the answer.

"They didn't sleep at home," John says, getting up. "I've got to help the other parents be diplomatic or war with the Germans will actually start," John adds.

John was leaving Jane's room when she asks him, "Dad, Heinz invited me on a picnic at the waterfalls. May I go?"

"Alone?" John asks.

Jane realizes she needs to tell her father the truth or she won't be able to go.

"No, Dad, I won't be alone. He invited the girls as well."

"Yes, but the girls disappeared, remember?" John enquires, realizing that Jane knows where the girls are.

"The picnic will be this afternoon. Maybe they'll show up by them," Jane completes, lowering her head.

John closes the door of her room and sits back down on the bed.

"What makes you think that? Jane, do you know something I don't?" John queries.

Before she could answer, a lot of shouting is heard, which makes Jane, Margaret, and John run to the stairs.

"We were looking for her… Ah, there you are, Jane!" Sarah exclaims, pointing at Jane.

"Dad, we spent all night searching for Jane," Agatha comments, looking Jane in the eyes.

They all look at Jane in rebuke.

"I'm sorry, girls. I couldn't find you and came back by myself," Jane replies, rather irritated. She immediately goes back into her room.

Everyone breathes a sigh of relief, the girls return to their rooms, and routines are reestablished.

John, on the other hand, still has his doubts, and goes into Jane's room. She was almost ready to go to breakfast.

"What happened yesterday, Jane?" John asks, taking a seat on the sofa.

"What I told you, Dad. I met Heinz and we danced and talked all night. He's a decent young man," Jane replies, trying to avoid this conversation and getting up to leave the room.

"Sit next to me, young lady. We're not through yet," John says, pointing at an empty spot on the sofa.

Jane realizes she won't be able to escape from her father and takes a seat.

"I don't want you to repeat what you've already told me. I'm here to listen to what you haven't told me," John adds.

"I... I," Jane stammers.

"I never thought I'd do this with you, Jane, but if you don't tell me what you know, I'll prohibit you from going on that picnic and I'll order a soldier to follow you all day today. Is that what you want?" John asks.

"Dad, I hate gossips and... I don't see any benefit in telling what I saw or didn't see. They're okay and home. Isn't that enough?" Jane asks. "The other parents seem less interested in what happened than you are," Jane answers.

"The other parents think their daughters are angels. I know that only my daughter is, in fact, one. I want you to tell me, so I know for certain if I should send you back to England or not," John states.

"No, Dad, not that!" Jane says, distraught.

"Well, then. What happened? Wasn't that what you wanted most until yesterday?" John asks, smiling.

Jane feels awkward. She knows her father is right.

"Dad, I ... I really liked talking with Heinz. I know he's the enemy, but..."

Jane's father interrupts her.

"The enemy is not a German soldier, daughter. Of that, I'm certain. The enemy is for whom the soldier fights for. I've got nothing against this Heinz. In fact, I need to thank him for bringing my daughter home safely," John adds, making Jane start smiling. "Now, tell me what you know."

Jane realizes she won't be able to get away and tells her father everything she saw the girls doing.

He's shocked by the news but, when Jane finishes her story, John kisses her on the forehead and says," Forgive me for doubting your judgment, my child. You were more than right about those girls," John pauses and finishes. "I'm happy I have a sensitive and decent daughter who has values. I trust you even more, Jane."

John gets up from the couch and begins to leave Jane's room when she asks him, "Are you going to tell the other parents?"

"It wouldn't do any good. They're only going to hear what they want to," John replies.

"May I go to on the picnic, or do you no longer trust the girls?" Jane asks, troubled.

"I never trusted those girls. I've always trusted you and I still do. You may go to the picnic with them, not because I think you'll be safe with them, but because, with them, that soldier will know for certain my Jane is special," John justifies, smiling as he leaves her room.

Breakfast takes place normally. After eating, the men decided to play cards with the women and the girls pull Jane to the library.

"Yesterday was phenomenal," Agatha exclaims, full of joy.

"We almost got caught. Who knew the boys' quarters were so far away," says Tina.

"Why did you wait until dawn to return?" Jane asks.

"It was still dark when we left, but we got lost and time got away from us," Debby responds.

"I would have slept there forever, if it were up to me," Agatha adds.

"Didn't the boys know how to get to the base?" Jane asks.

"I don't know. Maybe. Who knows?" Sarah replies. "Why?"

"I thought you'd come back with them," Jane says.

"No, when we left, they went to bed. They were very tired," Agatha explains, smiling.

"Heinz brought me here," Jane says.

"Of course, he brought you. You didn't wear him out," Agatha responds, smiling.

"I even wanted to help him get tired, but he said he wanted to sleep," Agatha adds.

Jane is rather happy hearing that Heinz hadn't fallen for Agatha's charms. Jane thought she was the prettiest of the group.

"Did he say anything about the picnic?" Jane asks, trying to bring the subject up.

"Yes, he did. I loved the idea. The falls is lovely," Agatha responds.

"What will we take to eat?" Sarah asks.

"Oh, I don't know. Ask the cook to make something that's both delicious and an aphrodisiac," Agatha replies, smiling.

"I want to make a cake," Jane says. "I want him to see that I know how to do things by myself," Jane adds.

"But do you know how to cook?" Tina asks, smiling.

"No, but I can try," responds Jane.

"I'll ask the cook to make some sandwiches. I'm not going to mess up my nails in the kitchen," Agatha says, leaving the library.

"I'm going to get fixed up for the picnic. Who wants to go with me?" Sarah asks.

They all leave the library, except for Jane, who stays there looking for a book with cake recipes.

Since she didn't find any cookbooks in the library, Jane goes to the kitchen, where she's well received by the staff. Most of them like her sweet and gentle ways.

"Could you help me bake a cake?" Jane asks the cook.

"What kind of cake would you like me to make?" asks the cook, with a strong German accent.

"I don't want you to make it. I want you to teach me how," Jane asserts, putting an apron on.

"Okay, if that's what you want," says the cook.

Jane follows the cook's instructions, but since she was new at it, it took her a long time to finish the recipe.

"My God, I'm late!" Jane exclaims, looking at the clock. "I need to take a bath and get ready. Would you please put the cake in the oven for me and include it in the picnic basket?" Jane asks the cook, who quickly helps her.

Jane flies up the stairs and tries to fix herself up as best she can in a short amount of time.

Sarah rushes into Jane's room.

"We're late. Are you ready?" Sarah asks, noticing that Jane hasn't begun putting on any makeup.

"I'll just use a little lipstick and then I'll be ready," Jane responds.

Going down the stairs, she realizes the girls were dressed and their hair was done as if they were going to another dance.

"My God, girls! We're going on a picnic, not to a ball," Jane says, grabbing one of the picnic baskets.

"We should always look our best," Agatha responds, looking Jane over from top to bottom.

She says goodbye to her parents, who are playing cards. John looks at Jane, kisses her cheek, and whispers in her ear, "I'm not going to tell you to use your noggin, because you already do. Try to teach those girls to use theirs," John says, making Jane smile.

"Have fun, girls," Agatha's mother say, waving at all of them.

The waterfalls was further than the dance hall, about three kilometers from the base's entrance. Halfway there, Jane notices that her group begins walking slowly.

"What's happening, girls? Did you change your mind about going?", Jane asks.

"My feet are asleep," Sarah says.

"Maybe wearing high heels on a picnic isn't such a good idea," Jane responds, smiling.

"Button your lip, Jane. You're just jealous because we're prettier than you," Agatha shoots back, limping in her high heels.

"I really am green with envy," Jane replies, all smiles and bouncy in her comfortable shoes. "Why don't you use some common sense and take off your shoes?" Jane suggests.

"And ruin my stockings?" Agatha asks, who's now walking faster, because she was mad at Jane.

Normally, it would take no more than forty minutes, but the girls walked for an hour and a half, which made them really late.

Arriving at the falls, the girls immediately saw Heinz and the other soldiers who were smoking while they waited. The girls dropped their baskets and ran to meet the soldiers. Jane, however, worries about the food and tries to gather the baskets up off the ground. Heinz notices her concern and runs to help her with them.

"Good afternoon. How are you?" Heinz says, taking most of the baskets.

"I'm fine. And you? Were you able to get a little sleep?" Jane asks.

"Maybe an hour, I think. We got up early to break camp," Heinz responds. "Are you dressed the way you like today?" he asks, looking at Jane's shoes.

"More or less, I don't really like lipstick," Jane says, smiling.

"To me, you're prettier than you were yesterday," Heinz compliments her.

"When your feet don't hurt, you have a nicer smile," Jane jokes. "And your feet? How are they?"

"They said they'll have to amputate them because of the gangrene, but I'll live," Heinz says smiling.

"Are you leaving? Is that why you took down your camp and are in uniform?" Jane asks.

"I really don't know. I just know that they told us to dismantle our camps... We'll have a meeting later," he replies, helping Jane. "As for the uniform... it's the only clothes we have," Heinz explains smiling.

The places were set, and everyone ate their sandwiches quickly, since it had been a long walk for everyone and they were all hungry.

When it was time for desert, Jane happily served her cake. She handed the first slice to Heinz.

"I made this cake myself," Jane said proudly.

Before trying her cake, Jane notices that all of them are making strange faces, except Heinz, who continues eating quickly.

"What was it? Don't you like chocolate cake?" Jane asks, putting the first bite in her mouth and then immediately spitting it out. "My God! That's horrible! I must have used salt instead of sugar," Jane exclaims, drinking her juice quickly.

"You think?" Agatha asks maliciously.

Everyone throws their cake into an improvised trash bag and sits next to the waterfalls, leaving Heinz and Jane alone to clean up the mess.

"You ate it all?" Jane asks, surprised at his attitude.

"Yes, I did," says Heinz, wiping away a tear and smiling at Jane.

"My God! That was an unnecessary sacrifice. Even I didn't eat it," Jane comments, smiling.

"I think it's a custom. Every time my mother cooked, my father ate everything," Heinz justifies.

"Ah, but she must know how to cook," Jane concludes, closing the baskets.

"I think she always got the salt and sugar right. She was smart. She bought two pots, one labeled 'salt' and the other 'sugar'," Heinz says, smiling.

She begins throwing sticks and leaves at Heinz, who doesn't return fire. He just smiles.

"Did your father scold you for getting home late," Heinz asks.

"No, he didn't see me arrive," Jane replies.

"I'll bet he saw your friends arrive!" Heinz says, smiling.

"They got there this morning, didn't you know?" Jane asks.

"They left after sunrise, so they probably arrived after sunrise," he explains.

"But they said it was still dark when they left," says Jane, confused.

"Do you want to know what happened?" Heinz asks.

Jane shakes her head yes and he continues.

"I left you at the mansion and ran to the base's entrance. The sun still hadn't come out when I got back to the camp, but your friends were still making a lot of noise. I decided to sleep outside the camp and was going to the car when your friend came after me," Heinz says, being interrupted by Jane.

"It was Agatha, wasn't it?" Jane asks.

"I don't know their names, but it was the blond," Heinz confirms. "Her name isn't important, because, in part, I don't think you should hang out with them," Heinz pauses. "I don't know if you're going to believe me, but your 'friend' was naked when she came up to me and asked if I wanted to 'have some fun'."

"She told me she'd tried something with you, but she isn't my 'friend'," Jane says, lowering her head.

"Did she tell you that I told her I was sleepy?" Heinz asks, distraught.

"Yes, she did, and I'll admit it made me happy," Jane confirms.

"What? Were you jealous?" Heinz asks, smiling.

"No, I just thought you could do better than her," Jane lies, smiling. "Did you see what time they left?" Jane asks, changing the subject.

"I got in the car and tried to sleep, but the sun was coming up and I knew I'd have to get up soon. I left the vehicle and threw them out," Heinz says.

"My idea was that my soldiers would take them home and I even talked to them in German, but they said they had to sleep and that your companions knew how to take care of themselves. I think they deserved to go home alone, since their behavior wasn't that of wholesome girls, and they hadn't earned much consideration." Heinz pauses. "But they left, and the sun was coming up, which is why I think I slept an hour."

"Poor thing, I feel sorry for you," Jane says, looking at him.

"I think a kiss would give me some energy," Heinz suggests, smiling.

Jane smiles, takes his hand and kisses it.

"Do you feel better?" Jane asks.

"It was a good start," Heinz says, smiling.

When it starts getting dark at the waterfalls, Heinz remembers their meeting.

"Lads, we need to go!" Heinz shouts. "Excuse me, Jane, but we really have to go. I'll take you to the base," he tells Jane.

The soldiers begin to say goodbye to the girls when Heinz interrupts them.

"We'll leave the girls at their base and then we'll go!" he exclaims, grabbing all the now empty baskets.

"Are you crazy, Heinz? We'll walk over five kilometers if we take them! Let them go by themselves. If they found their way here, they can find it back," one of the soldiers proposes.

"I'm just going to say this one time. We're taking the girls to the British base. Are you questioning my orders?" Heinz says with his command voice.

Jane notices the soldiers lower their heads and obey Heinz, without questioning his orders.

The soldiers follow in a rather foul mood. Heinz and Jane were out front, smiling and talking about literature. The other girls tried talking to their soldiers, but they didn't answer. They were merely obeying orders.

They were a few meters from the British base when Heinz heard something. He dropped the baskets and yelled "Duck!"

When everyone crouches, they feel the enormous crash of a bomb falling. The alarm at the British base begins to sound and many soldiers begin moving about.

Heinz knows very well what that sound is. He takes Jane's hand and shouts, "Run! Take cover!"

Before he could finish his phrase, the German army invades the British base, firing without mercy. At that moment, Heinz and his fellow soldiers' German uniforms made no difference. In all of the confusion, they were in enemy territory and were, thus, the enemy.

Another bomb is heard. Agatha and her soldier, who were furthest behind the group, are hit by the bomb and fall to the ground, lifeless. Jane, terrified, squeezes Heinz's hand, who finds a rock where they can take cover.

"Stay down!" Heinz tells Jane, who is panicking.

"They killed Agatha!" Jane exclaims, upset and crying.

"Stay quiet!" Heinz orders Jane.

He observes his soldiers running, abandoning the girls, who, lost, are crying and shouting.

"Get out of there! You're in the line of fire!" Heinz shouts.

While he's shouting, another bomb explodes near the girls. Shrapnel enters Sarah's leg, now desperate from the pain. Heinz starts to leave where they're hidden when Jane grabs him.

"Don't abandon me!" she says, crying.

"I'd never do that!" Heinz exclaims, crouching. "I need to go to her, Jane. Your friend's bleeding badly," he adds.

Jane understands the situation and releases Heinz, who runs to Sarah.

"Come on, girls, follow me!" says Heinz, carrying an unconscious Sarah.

He takes Tina and Debby to the rock, where Jane is trembling from fear. Because he's a little more experienced, Heinz examines the wound in Sarah's leg and realizes she's bleeding out.

"The shrapnel hit an important vein. You need to stop the blood loss, or she'll die quickly," Heinz explains to Jane who immediately uses her scarf to bind Sarah's leg, reducing the bleeding.

"What's happening?" Debby asks, upset.

"I don't think we accepted the English terms. We're at war!" says Heinz, taking his pistol out.

"Are you going to kill us?" Tina asks.

"If I wanted to, you wouldn't be here," Heinz replies, observing his surroundings.

"I think Sarah's dead," Jane says, trying to help her anyway she could.

Heinz looks at Sarah's leg and sees that it's covered in blood. Jane's scarf wasn't enough to stop the bleeding. He then touches Sarah's neck, looking for her pulse, but doesn't find one.

"She is, Jane. I'm sorry," Heinz confirms.

"We're all going to die!" Debby screams hysterically, standing up from their hiding place.

"Get down!" Heinz orders.

"What good will it do? We're surrounded!" Tina adds.

"I'll get you out of here and leave you at the mansion. It's fortified. That way you'll have a chance," Heinz replies.

Jane, completely traumatized, was holding the cloth soaked in Sarah's blood, who was now pale.

"Let's go, Jane. We need to move!" Heinz says, holding her hand.

Jane was still in shock and a sound of another explosion awoke her from a deep trance.

"I'm not going to leave you. Trust me. I'm going to take you to your father… Let's go," he says, pulling Jane.

Some German soldiers pass in front of Heinz and, in the confusion of noise and ash, threaten to shoot at the group. Heinz, without thinking or hesitating, shoots three German soldiers and takes their weapons.

Jane cannot believe the level of violence. She, who did not know what hatred, rage, or combat were, was living experiences that only existed in her books.

Heinz defended the girls from everything and everyone that threatened them like a wild wolf. He fought under no flag that afternoon. His only mission was to get Jane to her father.

Tina and Debby tried to reach Heinz and Jane, but with their shoes, it was impossible. Seeing their difficulties, the girls decide to take them off, which further increased the distance between the girls and Heinz.

"Stop, Heinz, the girls are falling back," Jane shouts, pulling his arm.

He looks at them and notices two German soldiers approaching them from behind. Before Heinz can aim, both shoot at Debby, who falls lifeless on the ground. Tina, desperate, runs toward Heinz, who hits one of the soldiers in the head. The second soldier is shot by an English soldier who then aims at Heinz. Jane pulls Tina to the ground and both duck, which increases Heinz's field of vision. He then shoots the English soldier.

"Debby, Jane…. Debby," Tina stammers, crying.

Jane's in deep despair and embraces Debby as best she can on the ground.

"Let's go, girls. We can't stop now!" Heinz shouts, looking all around.

"We just lost three friends in less than half an hour and you want us to run?" Tina asks, in despair.

"Jane, we can't stop," he says, looking at her. She stands up and takes both Heinz's and Tina's hands.

The trio continues running. Heinz does what he can to avoid increasing the group's terror with more deaths. Thus, he tries to move forward, hiding as well as he can.

Jane slips on a hill near the mansion and Heinz grasps her by the arm, keeping her from being exposed to a group of soldiers at the base of the hill. Trying to secure Jane, Heinz forgets about Tina and she falls near the soldiers.

Without realizing it was a woman, a soldier shoots Tina a point blank range. When he realizes that he's shot a woman, the soldiers run from the scene, leaving her lifeless body on the ground.

"They killed Tina... she slipped because of me," Jane says, in despair.

Heinz doesn't say anything. He just embraces Jane and waits for the group to leave.

"I'm out of ammunition. We'll have to be careful," Heinz cautions, releasing Jane and taking her hand.

They're near the mansion when Heinz finds the body of a soldier and takes his pistol.

"Look, Heinz, the mansion," Jane says, pointing. "Where is it?"

Heinz says nothing, which makes her even more desperate.

"Where's the house, Heinz?"

"Calm down, Jane. They probably evacuated the house in time," Heinz responds.

Both of them reach the mansion, which, by then had been completely destroyed.

"Jane, we'll hide in the ruins until the attack ends," Heinz says, pulling her.

An English soldier spots Heinz, identifies him as German, and fires. The bullet grazes Heinz's leg and he falls. Jane ducks from the sound of the gunfire and sees Heinz on the ground, immobile.

The English soldier believes he's hit Heinz and runs toward him to check if, in fact, he had. When he gets a little closer, Heinz, still on the ground, aims at and hits the English soldier.

"My God! You're bleeding!" Jane observes, ripping a piece of her dress and using it to staunch the bleeding.

Before she places the cloth on him, Heinz looks at his wound and says, "The bullet just grazed me. We need to hide," standing up with her help.

Heinz finds a safe, hidden place and lies down next to Jane.

"We'll stay here until the attack ends," Heinz repeats, holding his leg.

"My parents, Heinz? Where are my parents?" Jane says, crying.

"Stay calm, Jane. I'm sure they must have gotten out in time. When the attack ends, they'll return," Heinz responds, breathing with difficulty due to the pain.

"Are you all right?" Jane asks, worried.

"I'm tying my wound tightly, which makes it hurt more. That's all," Heinz says, now breathing normally.

"Are you sure my parents will come back here?" she asks.

"No, Jane, I don't know for certain, but I hope so," Heinz states.

Jane observes Heinz's wound. Even though it was deep, he's stopped losing blood.

"It's not bleeding anymore," Jane says.

"Jane, I ... I shot German soldiers," Heinz says and begins to cry.

His vulnerability makes Jane overcome the fear she'd felt up until that moment and embraces him.

"You were saving your own life, too. They didn't see your uniform... It was in legitimate self-defense," she justifies, kissing Heinz's head.

He calms down and begins to guard their hideout.

"How long will the attack last?" Jane inquires.

"I don't know, Jane. I think I missed the meeting about the attack," Heinz replies.

"It's my fault," Jane says, covering her face with her hands and crying. "You'd be all right if I hadn't gotten in your way."

"Jane, you didn't make me do anything and I have no regrets about having stayed with you," Heinz affirms.

"How will we know the attack is over?" Jane asks.

"When you stop hearing bang bang and boom boom, it'll be because it's over," Heinz says, smiling, trying to calm her down.

"My friends died right before my eyes, my parents are missing, and you're making a joke?" Jane questions angrily.

"I'm sorry, I thought I could ease some of the tension," Heinz says, removing Jane's hands from her face. "I thought those girls were your companions, not your friends!" Heinz adds.

"Friends or companions, they didn't deserve that end," Jane states.

"No one deserves it, Jane. No one," Heinz replies.

# Chapter XII

Jane and Heinz have been hidden in the rubble for an hour. Distraught, she looks all around, searching for her parents. He, in turn, takes care of his wound so it won't start bleeding again.

"Heinz, you're pale," Jane observes, looking at his wound again.

"I've lost a lot of blood. That must be why," Heinz replies. "I don't hear any guns. I think the attack's ended," he signals, standing up to look around.

"Do you think we can look for my parents now?" she asks, supporting Heinz.

"Yes, Jane, we'll look but we need to be fast, since our army will send in a unit to reconnoiter, and I don't know what they'd do with us," Heinz stresses, now walking on his own.

"You're wearing a German uniform. They won't do anything. I'm the problem," Jane replies, looking at the ruins of the house.

"I know. I'm thinking about what to say," Heinz pauses and continues. "Jane, if your parents didn't get evacuated in time, there's a chance …" He hesitates before continuing.

"I know, Heinz. I'm not that naïve," Jane says, continuing to look everywhere.

"Imagine that the mansion still exists. Where were your parents the last time you saw them?" Heinz asks, trying to be rational.

"They were playing cards in the gazebo," Jane remembers, running to the garden.

Heinz tries to follow her, but his leg wound is really bothering him. He watches Jane, who suddenly stops.

"The gazebo was here," Jane points, shocked to see the locale destroyed.

Seeing the gazebo destroyed, Heinz takes Jane's hand, expecting the worst.

Getting closer, they spot a shocking scene of body parts scattered everywhere. From what he sees, Heinz concludes that the attack took place with no warning, which would have surprised the British army, facilitating the assault.

From the bodies' positions, Heinz could see that there had been a frustrated attempt to flee. "Jane's parents probably didn't survive," he thinks to himself.

"Jane, it might be better if I..." Heinz is unable to finalize his sentence, hearing Jane scream and cry, kneeling on the ground.

"No... no!" she repeats, crying desperately.

Heinz approaches and tries to take her from the scene. Her parents, as well as other bodies, were lying on the ground, mutilated. Jane point to her father's head and then to a back, still dressed, that she knew was her mother.

Jane kneels on the ground again and sees a hand with a gold ring, which she readily recognizes as being her mother's because she always wore it.

"Let's go, Jane. I think you've seen enough," Heinz suggests, approaching her.

"I should have died with them... why?" Jane asks, trembling and crying.

"Let's leave, Jane. Life goes on. You have to be strong," Heinz says, trying to calm her and lift her from the ground.

"Heinz, I want that ring. It's my mother's and has our family coat of arms on it. My father gave it to her on her birthday. Get the ring for me, I can't do it... Get it, please," Jane pleads, stammering and crying in despair.

"It's just jewelry, Jane. You'll suffer every time you look at it," Heinz says.

"I want to take it back to England, since I won't be able to bury them," she replies, trying to pull herself together.

Heinz realizes the ring's very important to her, so he leaves Jane for a moment and approaches Margaret's hand, which was partially covered by rubble.

Being as respectful as possible, he works to remove the ring from Margaret's hand and then covers Jane's parents' back and torso with some nearby debris.

"Now, Jane, I've got the ring. Here," Heinz says, handing her the jewelry.

The ring was large, and the family coat of arms was set off by precious stones. It was the only material good from her parents that Jane inherited at that moment and, for her, that jewelry had no monetary value.

She immediately places the ring on her finger and promises herself that she'll take it to England.

"Thank you," she says to him.

Heinz decides to return to his camp where he was with his soldiers were before everything happened. He knew he should leave, or he'd have to fight again. Avoiding where they'd be easily seen, Heinz leaves the British base and, in the woods, proceeds to the camp.

Reaching their destination, he sees it's exactly the way he and his soldiers had left it.

The tents were duly folded and placed in their vehicle. He, in turn, doesn't seem interested in the tents and looks for something else. Janes had been silent since leaving the gazebo's ruins.

He constantly observes her and remains quiet out of respect for the memory of her loved ones.

Heinz finally seems to find what he's looking for, a chest he places on the ground, and opens it quickly. He pulls a box and some cans from it.

Without saying anything to Jane, Heinz lights a fire and tries to heat up the cans. While the cans heat up, he opens a box in which Jane spots a small first aid kit.

"Help me, please," Heinz asks, handing a package to Jane.

She takes the package and begins to clean Heinz's wound as best she can. He twists in pain without making a sound.

"You need to close the wound," Heinz says.

"How do I do that?" Jane asks, speaking for the first time.

"There's a needle and thread in the box. Take them and sew up the wound," he directs her, rolling up a cloth.

"I've never sewn anything before," Jane says, anguished.

"It's really simple, Jane. Just do this," Heinz says, moving his hands, showing her how to sew.

"I'm not the right person to do this. Why don't you?" Jane asks, agitated.

"I'm going to feel a lot of pain. It'd be better if somebody else do it. Help me, please," Heinz pleads, looking into Jane's eyes, who has moved next to him.

Realizing she has no way out, Jane begins stitching up Heinz's wound. He bites on the cloth, to keep himself from yelling.

"Done!" Jane exclaims, cutting the line, feeling relieved.

"Inject me with this," Heinz says.

"What is it?" Jane asks, holding the syringe.

"Penicillin. My hands are shaking. You need to do this for me," Heinz replies.

After the injection, Heinz stands up and removes the cans from the campfire.

"How did you know you needed to do that with your wound?" Jane asks, curious.

"We learn basic first aid in the army," Heinz explains, opening one of the tins.

"What's that?" Jane questions, pointing to the can.

"It's food... That's the best thing I can say about it," he says smiling, handing her one and a spoon.

"Isn't the can hot?" Jane asks, hesitating to touch it.

"No, I didn't put it directly in the fire. I just left it close enough to warm it a little. You can eat it," Heinz says.

"I'm not hungry," Jane says, without touching the container.

"Jane, I know it looks horrible, but it's not all that bad," Heinz replies, offering the food once more.

"After everything I've seen today, I don't have any stomach for food," Jane justifies, with her eyes tearing up.

"Jane, I can imagine how you're feeling right now... A lot happened in a very short period of time and the shock must be terrible for you," Heinz says, putting Jane's food next to her. "I'm sure your parents, wherever they may be, want you to keep on living. Look... Your day's been full of emotions and your body's weak. You need to nourish yourself. If you don't want to eat for yourself, imagine that you're eating for your parents. Fight for your life. That way, you'll be respecting what they'd want," he adds.

Jane knew Heinz was right, and, in fact, her body was weak. Overcoming her feelings, Jane begins to eat the canned meal. She makes a face when she puts the first portion in her mouth.

"It tastes like smashed wieners," he says, smiling. "I wonder if there's any cake left?" Heinz asks, joking with Jane.

They both begin to laugh, and Jane loosens up.

"We're going to sleep here tonight," Heinz says, getting two sleeping bags. "It won't be cold. We can sleep without a tent, close to the fire."

She agrees, puts her bag close to his and lies down.

"You're not going to abandon me, are you?" Jane asks, looking at the stars.

"No, I'm not. I have a plan," he replies.

Jane looks at Heinz and notices that he's looking at her.

"Thanks for staying with me," Jane says.

"Being with you is a pleasure," Heinz asserts.

They both turn and go to sleep.

# Chapter XIII

Heinz wakes up very early and fixes breakfast while Jane sleeps on. He checks his wound, which seems drier and less painful.

Jane smells the breakfast he's prepared and gets up, agitated, looking for him.

As Heinz is out of her line of sight, she begins to cry hysterically because she can't find him. She immediately imagines he's given up on staying with her.

He materialized from the trees when he hears her crying and, anguished, asks, "What was it Jane? Did you see something? Did you have a nightmare?" Heinz asks.

Jane spots him and immediately stops crying.

"I thought you'd abandoned me," she responds, getting out of the sleeping bag.

"No, I… I just went to the bathroom," Heinz says, with a slight smile on his face.

"I need to go too. Where is it?" Jane asks.

Her question makes Heinz laugh loudly and, when he manages to stop chuckling, he responds, "In this region, we have a vast number of options," Heinz says, pointing to the trees. "To the right, we have a pine tree, or almond bathroom… It's your choice," Heinz observes her expression and decides to answer seriously. "Go straight that way. There's a small river that will serve you well as a toilet."

Jane realizes how ridiculous her question was, given the situation. She lowers her head and begins walking in the direction Heinz had pointed.

"I'm sorry. I needed to laugh a little. You've never been camping before, have you?" Heinz asks.

"No, I've never slept away from my parents," Jane replies. Remembering her parents, her eyes fill with tears.

"We need to leave soon. Go use the 'toilet' and I'll serve a bit of breakfast."

They're both ready to get in the Kubelwagen and leave when Heinz notices his soldiers' backpacks and clothes.

"What is it, Heinz?" Jane asks.

"My friends. I... I wonder if I shot them without realizing it?" Heinz queries, confused.

"I don't remember them after the first explosion. I just remember that soldier with Agatha, but he's the only one I saw. The others disappeared," Jane responds, putting her hand on his shoulder.

"They fled and rejoined the German army. I saw that and even understood it. They were right to do so," Heinz remembers.

"And why didn't you?" Jane asks, anxious about his answer.

"I'm sure you're smart enough to know the answer," Heinz says, placing his friends' backpacks against a tree.

"You're not going to take them?" Jane asks, pointing at the packs.

"They might return and will need their supplies. This way they'll know that I was here and have left," Heinz responds, getting into his vehicle.

Jane then gets in and holds Heinz's hand.

"Thanks for staying. I really appreciate your respect for me," Jane says, kissing Heinz's hand softly. He just smiles at her.

The two of them travel for a few hours until they reach a small village. Heinz then stops their car and chats in German with some people in the street who point toward a store. He returns to the Kubelwagen, where Jane was waiting and asks, "Do you trust me now?"

Jane nods her head yes and he continues, "I need to buy some German clothes for you, but if you speak in English, we'll immediately be suspect. When I show you a dress or clothes, shake your head if you like it or not, okay?" Heinz says, looking at Jane.

"But ... if she talks to me, asks something?" Jane questions.

"She isn't going to talk to you. I'll tell her that your mute and shy," Heinz replies, parking the vehicle in front of the store.

"I don't need clothes," Jane says.

"Yes, you do. For my plan to work, you will," Heinz says.

"Then anything you choose will be fine. I've never really cared about that. I just don't want high heels," Jane says.

He smiles and nods in agreement to her.

Entering the shop, Heinz, very friendly, chats in German with the shopkeepers who scurry to help him. They show Jane several dresses and other articles of clothing. She observes all Heinz's movements and obeys without speaking.

After trying on some clothes and constant dialogues in German between Heinz and the shopkeepers, a small feminine wardrobe is assembled for her. In a brief moment when both of them are alone together, Jane whispers in Heinz's ear, "How are we going to pay for this?"

"I've got some money. Go back to the car and wait there," he responds softly.

Heinz returns to the vehicle carrying a trunk, which he stores in the back.

"Where are the clothes?" Jane asks, when Heinz gets in the car.

"They're in the trunk. I want it to look like you're travelling," Heinz says.

"But I am," Jane replies, smiling.

He also smiles, and they continue their journey. Jane avoids speaking with Heinz. In deep silence, she reflects on her life, who she was and what it will be like from this day on. Fear and anguish were the feelings that most assailed her desolated heart.

Lunchtime comes, and Jane's hungry, but she doesn't want to ask Heinz for food; she was too proud to admit he was her sole source of survival at that moment.

Lunchtime had come and gone, and it was beginning to get dark; Jane's stomach was making noise, and Heinz continued their trip without chatting with her.

The sun was now setting when Jane puts her hand on her stomach; she was so famished it had begun to ache. She'd never felt that hungry before.

Heinz notices the movement of her hand to her stomach and begins to chuckle.

"What's so funny?" Jane asks angrily.

"So, you're really not going to ask me for food?" Heinz inquires, grinning.

"Are you playing around with me?" Jane turns to face Heinz, even more upset.

"Sometimes you remind me of my mother, upset and angry for no reason at all," he says, chortling while he pulls off to the side of the road.

Heinz gets out of the vehicle and opens the trunk in the back, takes out a paper sack and returns to the driver's seat.

"You can eat this," Heinz says, taking two sandwiches and a bottle of water out of the sack.

"Where did you buy this?" Jane questions, devouring her sandwich.

"While you were changing clothes, I asked the shop owner to buy some sandwiches for me," Heinz replies, smiling broadly.

"You knew I was starving, you had to be hungry yourself, but you preferred to not give me the sandwiches and just watch me?" Jane asks furiously.

"I'm used to going hungry. I wanted to see how proud you were," Heinz says, still grinning.

After a few minutes of silence, she still isn't satisfied and continues the argument.

"I'm not proud. I just didn't want to interfere with the trip," Jane says, who little by little finds the humor in his joke and also breaks out a slight smile.

"So, you're not proud, my rebellious little English princess?" Heinz mocks, finishing up his sandwich.

"Shut up, Heinz. I'm going to the facilities," Jane says, getting out of the Kubelwagen before disappearing into the woods.

He waits in the vehicle, grinning to himself.

They continue travelling and, after Heinz's joke, Jane loosens up a little and decides to break the silence.

"Where are we going?" Jane asks.

"Someplace safe," Heinz responds.

"Why don't you leave me at a port, so I can catch a boat back to England?" she questions.

"We're at war. The safest place in Europe right now is Germany," Heinz says.

"I can't stay here. There's nothing for me here," Jane states, lowering her head.

"Is there anything for you back in England?" Heinz inquires.

She knew she had nothing in either country. She didn't answer Heinz.

"Don't worry. You have me. I'll take care of you," Heinz responds.

"Thanks" was all she managed to say to him at that point. Her heart was beating rapidly, but it was the first time she'd felt safe since her parents had been killed.

It was night when Jane spotted a strong light in front of their vehicle. She immediately realized it was a military base.

"Are you going to turn me into the German army?", Jane asked, worried because she knew that being the daughter of an enemy colonel was a risk for her.

"If I had wanted to do that, I already would have. What do I have to do for you to trust me?" Heinz asks, irritated.

She apologizes for being afraid and decides to let Heinz take care of her.

"I didn't mean to doubt you," Jane responds, lowering her head.

Heinz then stops the car next to some German soldiers, who immediately walk toward them.

"Don't say anything until we're alone," Heinz says.

Jane shakes her head yes and remains silent.

The soldiers approach the Kubelwagen. Heinz grins and begins to say something in German. They also grin, and he points to Jane's trunk.

The soldiers lower their weapons. Heinz turns to Jane, says something in German, signally for her to stay in the car. Jane nods her head yes, Heinz leaves the vehicle and continues talking to the soldiers.

Jane watches him go to his backpack and remove some papers that he shows to a soldier who nods his head in agreement. Two soldiers then search Jane's trunk.

After a while, the soldiers open the gate for Heinz, who drives to a large house in silence.

During their drive to the house, Jane realizes that the base is well guarded by soldiers and that there were several small houses, some with children's toys in their tiny front yards. The structures were all identical and well organized.

"Oh, my. This base is much nicer that the British one," Jane thinks.

Heinz motions for Jane to get out of the vehicle, which she quickly does. He then takes her hand and walks into the large house. As soon as Heinz enters, he's received by a man, who is about 60 years old, duly uniformed with many medals on his chest. Heinz seems to know the man, who smiles upon seeing him.

He then let go of Jane's hand and offers to shake the gentleman's hand. He promptly gives Heinz an affectionate hug who returns it awkwardly.

Heinz points to Jane and the man shakes his head and smiles at her. She returns his smile.

Both are invited to enter a large room where an abundant supper is being served.

Heinz pulls a chair out for Jane. She self-consciously and shyly takes a seat at the table.

There are several women in the room, as well as men, and all the women began to smile and speak with Jane, who only smiles back without responding. Heinz then says something in German to the women. They then stop talking to her but continue smiling in a very friendly manner.

Jane finishes her meal, and everyone stands up and retires in a room with an enormous fireplace. Heinz sits next to Jane and delicately kisses her face, which provokes much laughter and many comments from the women's. From their gestures, she realizes his kiss makes those women's a little jealous, as they complain to those who apparently are their spouses.

The night transpires in a festive and happy mood. For Jane, nevertheless, it was a night filled with false smiles and extreme boredom.

Finally, the evening ends and Heinz seems to say good night to everyone. Jane copies his gestures and they both return to the vehicle.

When the car begins moving again, Jane, desperate, speaks with Heinz.

"What was that? Where are we? Why did we need to dine there?"

"Calm down, Jane. We're going home. I'll explain everything to you there," Heinz replies, while seeming to look for something with a paper in his hand.

"If you tell me what it is, I can help you," Jane responds anxiously.

"You don't need to. We've arrived!" he states, parking in front of a house.

Heinz takes out a key, which Jane had seen the gentleman give him before they left. It opens the door to a small house.

She goes inside, and her curious eyes observe everything. The house is small and simply furnished with a few things, but it has everything a basic home needs. There were a kitchen, two bedrooms, a bathroom and a living room with a fireplace, a couch, and a radio. Out back, she saw a small yard with a clothes line and a small sink for washing laundry. After surveying it all, Jane returned to the living room, where Heinz was sitting on the couch, waiting for her with his boots off.

"Where are we?", Jane begins.

"This is a military base for soldiers and their families," Heinz responds.

"Can any soldier live in these houses?"

"No, just soldiers who've been invited to," he replies.

"Did you live here before?"

"No, it's for families. I had no reason to live here. I preferred the battlefield. I've never liked working in the rear echelon," Heinz says.

"How did you get this house then?"

"I received a letter inviting me to live here a month ago. I was going to throw the letter out, but decided to keep it," Heinz says.

"Why did they invite you?"

"I was promoted to sergeant and they gave me a few men to command," Heinz responded, making a small pause.

"What do you mean?" Jane inquired, anxiously.

"You met the men I commanded. I think they're dead," he added, with grief.

"I'm sorry, Heinz," Jane also pauses, but is still curious. "You were promoted, and they gave you the letter?"

"I was promoted, and my uncle found out. My uncle is the man with the medals, in the large house. His name is Claus Baurmann, and the woman with him is his wife, Nina Baurmann. He commands this base and didn't want me fighting in the field. He sent me a letter and offered me a position in the intelligence service, analyzing messages, which is why he sent me the letter," Heinz replies.

"And what did you tell them about me?" Jane asks.

"Your name now is Frida. That's what I told them, so I won't be calling you Jane any more. That's very important," Heinz explains.

"Why Frida?" Jane asks.

"Because Jane is very British," he replies. "I told them you're mute and very shy, which is why the women left you alone."

"How long do you think they'll believe this farce"" Jane grills Heinz.

"How long will it take you to learn to speak German?" Heinz asks her with a smile.

"Are you going to teach me?" Jane asks.

"Your first lesson will be tomorrow. We're going to sleep now. I'm exhausted," Heinz says.

He enters one of the two rooms. Jane realizes that her trunk is in the other room. She then enters her new room and quickly falls to sleep without even taking her clothes off.

# Chapter XIV

The next morning, Heinz gets up early and leaves the house. Frida wakes up a few hours later and decides to surprise him with breakfast.

She realizes there's no food in the house and suspects that Heinz has left to get some.

Half an hour after she wakes up, he appears with sacks and books.

"I tried to make breakfast, but I didn't find any food," Frida says, following Heinz.

"I bought some stuff. I also took advantage of being out and went to the base library to pick up a few books for you," Heinz replies, putting the provisions in the kitchen.

Seeing the books, Frida moves close to him to get them.

"Heavens, I've been dying for something to read!" she exclaims, leafing through the pages. "But these books are in German?" Frida asks, disappointed.

"Do you think there's any other kind on the base?" Heinz inquires, chuckling. "These are children's books. We can start with them." And he points to a chair at the table.

He then begins teaching Frida the German alphabet. She shows great interest and curiosity about the language.

The week goes by quickly. Both of them rarely leave the house. Heinz dedicates himself completely to teaching Frida some German.

There are several neighbors around the house, many of them with children. Frida, in her few intervals between lessons, spends her time observing the neighbors, their habits, the way they take care of their children, and anything else she sees as important in order to learn how to live there.

"Frida, we were invited to dinner tomorrow at the big house with my aunt and uncle. I can't ignore the invitation!" Heinz warns.

"No, we can't! They've been so generous!" Frida says.

"Supper Frida we go!" Frida adds, in German.

"Almost..." Heinz responds, smiling, in English. "Do you think you're ready to understand a little more of our conversations at the big house?" Heinz asks.

"I'll try," Frida says, in German.

"That was perfect!" he exclaims, smiling and lightly kissing Frida's cheek.

The next day, Frida wakes up early and tries to fix breakfast. Since she'd never had to, she did her best to copy what she'd seen Heinz cooking.

"Good morning," Frida says in German, seeing that Heinz had woken up.

"Good morning," Heinz responds, also in German. "What are we having for breakfast?" he continues, in German.

"Eggs, bread, milk, and toast," she says, still in German.

"Excellent, Frida. You learn fast!" Heinz responds in German.

He notices that the toast was burnt and, eating the eggs, that they needed salt.

"It seems like next week, we need to alternate German lessons with cooking lessons," Heinz sayings while chortling but still eating his breakfast.

Frida blushes after he speaks and tries her food.

"My God! I really am bad," Frida confirms, picking up the salt.

"It's better than the cake," Heinz adds, chuckling loudly.

She begins to laugh also and they both continue eating.

The sun has begun to set when Frida begins to get ready for supper. She chooses her best dress and spends a few hours in front of the mirror, trying to copy the hair she'd seen her neighbors wearing, as well as their makeup.

"We're going to be late," Heinz shouts, in German, at Frida's door.

"I'm now leaving," she responds in German.

"I'm leaving now," Heinz corrects her in German.

Jane exits her room and Heinz is impressed, as she has managed to pull off her hairdo and makeup perfectly."

"You're an authentic Frida," he complements, smiling.

Frida thanks him in German for the praise and the two get in the car on their way to the big house.

"I still don't feel ready to speak, Heinz," she states in English.

"I know that, Frida. I told my uncle that you and I are doing the exercises your doctor gave us, which is why I've been extremely busy helping you these days," Heinz says.

"Excellent idea. Do you think I'll ever be fluent?" Frida asks, excited.

"Fluent? Yes, I do. The problem is your accent. I must have a German accent in English. It's difficult to lose," Heinz replies.

"But your accent isn't strong. Maybe the same thing will happen with me," Frida says, lowering her head. "Do you think that I might not ever be able to talk with them?"

"I don't know yet. The best I can do is what I'm already doing. Let time take its course. Every now and then, I can make some excuse up or something like that," Heinz responds, trying to encourage her.

Frida and Heinz arrive punctually for dinner. Once again, Claus greets him very affectionately and gives Frida a huge hug, that makes her blush. Nina welcomes them both and takes Frida's hand, who grows desperate, being pulled by Heinz's aunt. He, in turn, motions for Frida to stay calm and listen.

Lost words and a few sentences are all that Frida manages to understand. From her gestures and expression, she concludes that Heinz's aunt is introducing her to the women there for dinner, who are all gathered near the fireplace.

Frida understands that the conversation was only for women, as Heinz tried to rescue her and was fiercely admonished.

Among the lost words, Frida identifies names of food and deduces that they're talking about what was for dinner. Among the few complete sentences that Heinz had taught her in a week were those in the form of a question, like, for example, "What do you think? Do you agree?" among other similar one that Heinz thought were necessary for Frida to know so she could nod her head.

Nina turns to her and uses one of the sentences that she knew, "What do you think, Frida?"

She had no idea what they were talking about, but notices everyone's happy faces and decides to shake her head "yes", which leads the group to an explosion of joy. Frida feels relieved, since her answer seems to satisfy the group.

Once again, Heinz, concerned, reappears and, this time, Frida understands the phrase, "Shall we eat?" She immediately stands up and takes Heinz's hand, who leads her to the table. Dinner proceeds calmly. Frida decides to imitate whatever expression Heinz uses; if he smiles or becomes quiet, she does the same.

During this dinner, Frida feels less lost. She understands very little but does manage to understand some things. Dinner ends and Heinz whispers in her ear, "Frida, start coughing. That way I can say you're coming down with a cold."

She waits a few minutes and begins to cough delicately. Heinz soon convinces the group to let them leave. His aunt, rather worried about Frida's cough, hands her a small bottle, which Frida realizes is cough syrup to be taken twice a day, according to instructions on the label. Heinz thanks her and they both leave the big house.

"Whew, I feel relieved," Frida says, now in the Kubelwagen.

"Me, too," Heinz responds. "It'll will be better if you either take the medicine or throw it away little by little. My aunt will be checking," Heinz continues, smiling.

"I need more books. I'm going to study more..." Frida says.

The days go by and each day she learns a little more of the language and those lost, missing words begin to make more sense. However, Heinz still does not let Frida talk to anyone, for her own safety.

He realizes that, bit by bit, Frida can now manage to study by herself, so he decides to return slowly to his activities in the army.

"Do you need to go every morning?" Frida asks unhappily.

"I'm still part of the army, Frida," Heinz says, putting on his boots. "I requested leave time to help you, but I've got a duty to fulfill," he adds.

"Do you know why you're fighting?" Frida asks.

"I'm not going to fight today, Frida. I've decided to accept the job my uncle offered, and I'm in a strategic job," he answers, turning to the door.

Heinz goes out for a few seconds and then comes back inside.

"Did you forget something?" she inquires.

He then steals a long, passionate kiss from Frida, who does not resist the kiss. However, because she's never kissed anyone before, she doesn't know what to do. Heinz removes his lips and looks at her. Embarrassed at not knowing what to do, she lowers her head. Heinz takes his hand from Frida's waist who still is hanging her head and leaves the house rather sad with his head also lowered.

"What did I do?" Frida asks herself, setting on the sofa. "Maybe it's because I've never done this and did nothing; that must be the problem," she finishes her thought and begins to cry.

Heinz returns home in the evening and finds Frida fixing supper.

"How was your day?" he asks her in German.

"It was normal," she responds, also in German.

The two spend a few minutes talking in German until a strong smell of something burning fills the house.

"The potatoes!" Frida says in English, running to the kitchen.

"If it's not burnt, it's not supper," Heinz adds, chuckling as he follows her.

"I'm so bad. Have you ever eaten anything I've done that was good?" Frida asks, sad.

"You heat milk up very well," Heinz replies, chuckling.

She begins to throw fruit at Heinz, who can't stop laughing.

"Look. That's awful, wasting food in a time of scarcity," he says, picking fruit up off the floor.

"Bloody hell, I ruined the potatoes and the sausage burnt, too," Frida confirms, shaking the pan to disperse the smoke.

"Do we have any beer?" Heinz asks.

Frida shakes her head yes and takes one from the refrigerator.

"Excellent. Beer will solve the problem," Heinz says.

"Do you think it'll taste better if I pour beer on it?" Frida asks, with the bottle still in her hand.

"Are you crazy? The beer's to help us eat," Heinz says, smiling, taking the beer from Frida's hand.

She begins to grin. Both of them sit down and force themselves to eat.

"It's better than the cake," Heinz remembers, smiling.

"You're going to remember that cake for the rest of your life, aren't you?" Frida inquires.

"Won't you?" Heinz asks, grinning. "We have another dinner at my uncle's."

Almost every weekend, they visit Heinz's uncle, and every week Frida learns more about the language and feels more secure at those dinners.

Heinz tries to talk to Frida about the kiss, but Frida changes the subject and tries her best not to respond to Heinz, who gets sad, but does not insist on the subject.

# Chapter XV

After visiting Claus and Nina's home so often, Frida has worn all of her dresses once and repeats one at the event, a faux pas she knows won't go unnoticed by a group of women.

"I'm wearing the same dress again," she tells Heinz.

"And... I've only got six sets of clothing and they're all the same. Don't you think I'm wearing the same clothes again from time to time?" Heinz asks, smiling.

"It's different. I'm a woman," Frida replies.

"Seriously? I'd never noticed that. Are you sure?" Heinz ironized, grinning.

"Stop joking. I'm serious," Frida says, irritated.

"Of all the women I've known, you're the last one I expected to hear say that," Heinz replies.

"The women will say something and I'm mute, remember?"

"Yes, and so what? What's the problem if they make comments. At least you should be happy that they're commenting in a language that you do not yet fully understand," Heinz replies.

"You need to defend me," Frida comments.

"That's no problem. When they talk about your dress, I'll slug one of them, and if they continue, I'll kick them," Heinz ironizes, still smiling. "I think it's a little aggressive, but if you insist…"

"You shouldn't be a soldier. You should be a circus clown," Frida tells him in German.

"Well, at least that phrase was correct," Heinz says, grinning.

As usual, she's welcomed by Claus and Nina, who discretely realizes that Frida has worn the dress before but says nothing. She only smiles. Frida blushes when she notices Nina looking at her dress, but before she can manage any other reaction, Heinz's aunt takes her arm and leads her into the house. Unlike the other times, she is taken to what seems like Nina's room because of the photos spread about.

Upon entering, Frida understands Nina's gesture to take a seat on the couch, which she does. Heinz's aunt goes into a closet and, after a few minutes, returns with a bridal gown.

"Frida, shall we see if this fits you?" Nina inquires.

Frida shakes her head no and tries to thank her with her gestures.

"But you said it wouldn't be a problem, remember? I had this dress sent from Munich. I hope it fits. If not, I'll have to do a lot of sewing," Nina says.

Frida tries to remember this question and her answer, but she can't and decides to keep her word and try the dress on.

"It must have been that day when I said yes but didn't know what for," Frida remembers while putting it on. "But why would she want to give me this dress? Could Heinz have said I'm going to get married?" Doubts fill Frida's head, which makes her dizzy and she trips.

"Be careful with the dress!" Nina shouts, taking hold of Frida's arm. "You're beautiful. It looks perfect. It just needs a few adjustments," she adds.

Frida is dazzled when she looks in the mirror. The last time she'd worn something so beautiful was when she went to the dance. She then remembers her mother and father, the gleam in their eyes that was similar to the one in Heinz's aunt's eyes.

"Why am I here? Why am I dressed like this?" Frida wonders.

"I'm sure Heinz will adore it," Nina says, fixing Frida's waist. "I've never met a fiancé like Heinz. He really loves you, you know? The last time I saw my nephew, he was surrounded by women at an army festival. I thought that boy'd never get married, but there you are… His eyes change when you arrive. It's sweet," she adds.

"Fiancé? He loves me? What does she mean?" Frida got more and more confused. She takes the dress off. There are so many doubts that Frida feels queasy with the situation and runs to the closest bathroom to throw up.

"Are you pregnant, dear?" Heinz's aunt asks happily.

Frida pulls herself together quickly and gestures emphatically that she's not pregnant, which makes Nina smile.

"We'll see, dear!" she smiles and exclaims.

Frida appears in the dining room, accompanied by Heinz's aunt.

Frida is pale and still rather confused. Heinz notices her features and runs to her aid.

"Get me out of here," she whispers to him in German.

"We'll eat first and then go."

"Go where?" Clause inquires.

"Frida isn't feeling well," Heinz responds.

"Well, well. Is she talking now?" Claus asks happily.

"She's working really hard, but she still feels embarrassed about speaking in public, because she still has a lot of problems," Heinz corrects himself.

"That's nonsense. We're all family, my dear," Nina adds.

"She still has a lot to overcome. She confuses her sentences at times and really has to work hard on some words," Heinz says, agitated.

Frida eats very little while Heinz quickly wolfs down his plate. Before desert is served, they excuse themselves and leave the table at the big house.

"What happened?" Heinz asks, upset, in the car.

"My German must not be good enough," Frida responds, covering her face with her hands, very confused.

"Settle down; you're upset. We'll talk about this calmly at home," Heinz says, kissing her hand.

Arriving home, Frida quickly goes in and runs to her room. Heinz tries to follow her but realizes it'd be better to leave her alone for a few minutes. He then goes to the kitchen.

"Frida, I've made you some tea," Heinz says at the door to her room.

Heinz enters the room and sees Frida on the bed, with her eyes swollen from crying. He leaves the tea on the night stand near her and leaves her room without saying anything.

"We need to talk," Frida says to Heinz, who had begun to shut the door.

"I'm going to get a chair," he responds.

"There's no need to; come sit here," Frida says, leaving a space next her on the bed.

Heinz is surprised by Frida's request, since she's never let him sit on the bed before. Nevertheless, he obeys.

"Something happened with my aunt, right? Did she say something hurtful to you?" Heinz asks, already knowing the answer.

"Yes, something happened… I think," Frida pauses and continues. "Or maybe nothing happened, and I need to learn more German." Frida drinks a little of the tea. She's calmer now.

"What happened? Can you tell me what she said in German?" Heinz anxiously asks.

"She told me that we are engaged," Frida responds in German. "Engaged?" she repeats in English.

"Well, Frida," Heinz says, stammering.

"Am I right? Are we engaged?" she asks again.

"I had to do that," Heinz explains, not looking at her.

"How long have we been engaged?" Frida asks, seeking out his eyes.

"How long have we been here?" Heinz asks.

"Five months," Frida responds, noting that the time had gone by quickly. "I hadn't even noticed."

"Neither had I," Heinz states.

"So, all this time, I've been your fiancée?" Frida asks.

"Yes, my uncle's been trying to arrange the paperwork for our wedding, since I told him you'd lost your identity card," Heinz adds.

"How did I lose my identity card? Where was I born? What is my last name?" Frida asks, anxiously.

"I told him that you were from Munich. No one asked me your last name, since you'll have mine," Heinz answered.

"Why did we need to be engaged?" Frida asks.

"I could only bring you to the base if you were my wife. So, I told my uncle that I was going to marry you, but since you'd lost your identity card, I hadn't been able to make our marriage official," Heinz explains. "Which is why my uncle offered to help me."

"How did I lose my identity card?" Frida asks again.

"I didn't lie about that part. I told him that a bomb had hit your house, killing your parents, and, that, luckily, you weren't at home," Heinz responded.

"Your aunt showed me a bridal gown that I apparently let her give me as a present," Frida says.

"What? Why did you let her?" Heinz asks.

"Well, let me see..." Frida pauses, ironically. "Maybe it's because I was born in Manchester and I don't know how to speak German?" Frida says.

Heinz smiles a little.

"Is the dress pretty?" he asks.

"I don't know. I was trying so hard not to throw up on it. It was too much information for me all at once," Frida replies.

"Wow, did you throw up?" Heinz asks.

"Ah, yes. I have to finish by informing you that your aunt thinks I'm pregnant," Frida answer, drinking more tea.

"My, oh my. I really am good!" Heinz exclaims, chuckling.

"That's not funny. You should have told me," Frida responds.

"Would you have accepted?" Heinz says.

"No, but that's another story," she responds.

Heinz hears Frida's answer, becomes sad, and begins to walk toward the door. She realizes that she needs to do something at that very moment or she'll lose him.

"But I'll accept now if you tell me what you feel for me," she shouts, in German.

"What difference would that make? You've always seen me as a friend. I tried to tell you what I felt, but you avoid me," Heinz responds in English, crying.

"I don't know what to do. I've never dated before. I've never been with boys my age. My parents always protected me, and I spent most of my time at home," Frida says.

"You've never had a boyfriend?" Heinz asks, startled.

"You're the first boy I've danced with in my life. Does that tell you enough?" Frida adds lowering her head.

Heinz returns to the bed and lifts her head, looking deeply into her blue eyes.

"I love you," Heinz says, full of emotion.

"I love you, too," Frida responds, crying.

They begin to kiss each other, and Heinz places her hands around his neck. He then gently lies on the bed and begins to softly kiss her body. Frida surrenders to her feelings that have insisted on existing since she first met Heinz.

Realizing that Frida wanted the same thing he did, Heinz begins to gently remove her dress, but she moves his hand.

"I'm sorry. I thought you wanted to. I didn't mean to be so forward and..." Heinz says, begging forgiveness.

Frida kisses him again and responds, "I was startled, that's all."

She places Heinz hand back on her body and he begins kissing her again.

"Well, at least if I'm pregnant, the child will have an earthly father," Frida states, smiling.

"I thought I'd have to explain where babies come from... You know that storks have nothing to do with it, don't you?" Heinz says, jokingly.

"You don't need to explain it to me. You need to show me how it's done," Frida responds, hugging and kissing Heinz.

They surrender to one another and spend the night together.

# Chapter XVI

The next morning, Frida and Heinz wake up, embracing and in very good spirits.

"I think I need to go," Heinz says, kissing her.

"Stay a little longer. It's cold," she pleads, hugging him, keeping him from leaving.

"When you put your clothes on, you won't be cold any longer," Heinz replies, chuckling.

"And what if I don't want to?" Frida, retorts, provoking him.

"I'll love it, but you'll still feel very cold," Heinz replies, giving her another kiss. "I really need to go."

He struggles, managing to slip out of Frida's strong hug, and gets up from the bed. Frida, however gets up quickly as well and hides Heinz's clothes.

"Okay, I'll put your dress on, instead," he says, picking up her clothes. Frida smiles.

"You're going to rip my party dress," Frida replies.

"Give me my clothes back," Heinz pleads.

Frida says no, so he begins to put her dress on.

"You wouldn't have the nerve to go to work like that," Frida says, smiling.

"Of course not. I need the right footwear," Heinz agrees, looking for her shoes.

Frida realizes that Heinz is destroying her dress, since his broad shoulders keep him from zipping it up.

"Your butt's showing. You need to close the dress up," Frida says, laughing.

"It's the latest style in the army. I'm a pioneer," Heinz replies.

"Don't be silly and stop ruining my clothes. Here. Take yours," she says, handing him his uniform.

He then begins to dress correctly, and Frida says, "Leave the army. Let's go somewhere and start a family together," Frida pleads.

"Did you mother ever say that to your father?" Heinz asks, buttoning up his jacket.

"Whenever my father returned home, she always asked him not to go again," Frida responds.

"And what did he do?" asks Heinz.

"One day he came home and told us that he was going to take my mother and me to a military base," she adds.

"And what did I do?" Heinz replies, smiling.

"Our life can be different. I know how the story about my mother and father ended," Frida remembers, with tears in her eyes. "I don't want that for us."

"I can't leave the army," Heinz responds, almost dressed.

"Why not? Why do you insist on continuing to fight?" Frida asks in agony.

"Now, I'm fighting for you, for the family that I want to have with you, for a country where I can see my children grow up free," Heinz replies, kissing Frida on the cheek.

"And why do you think Germany is the best place for that? Why can't we go to England?" Frida inquires.

"Because if I leave the German army with all the information I have, they will shoot me for desertion, and if I went to England and they discovered I was in the German military, they'd shoot me for espionage," Heinz justifies.

"And if we fled to America?" Frida suggests.

"I don't want to spend the rest of my life fleeing. What kind of life would that be for you and our children? I'm not a coward. I'd rather fight," Heinz says.

"If you die, what happens to me? To our children?" Frida asks, crying.

"As far as I know, we don't have any children yet and, if you let me go train, I'll be good, and it will be hard for them to get me," Heinz responds, smiling. "I can't train in this room," Heinz adds.

Frida realizes it would be useless to continue arguing and, in fact, if Heinz trained, it'd be better for both of them. Fleeing seemed like a very risky thing to do for the rest of their lives.

A month goes by and Claus finally gets the papers for Heinz and Frida's wedding.

"We're going to hold the wedding next week," Claus communicates smiling and toasting.

By now, Frida risked conversing with everyone while pretending perfectly that she had a problem articulating her words.

"Come on, Frida, in honor of this moment, say something!" Nina encouraged her.

Frida stood up and took a glass of champagne.

"I'd like to thank everyone. I love my future husband very much," she says with difficulty in German.

Everyone smiles, especially Heinz, who is overflowing with happiness.

The week goes by quickly and their wedding day arrives.

To get ready, Frida spends the night at Claus's house, where his wife happily helps with all the preparations.

Everyone on the base was invited to the party, which Claus was paying for.

"Thanks for doing all this, uncle!" Heinz says.

"I'm doing this for you and for my sister," Claus states.

"Have you invited my mother?" Heinz asks anxiously.

"I've tried to talk to her ever since you arrived at the base, but I can't find her," he replies sadly.

"What do you mean? Has something happened to her?" Heinz questions worriedly.

Heinz is happy about marrying Frida, but now he seems worried.

The wedding takes place, and everyone is seated at a table for the reception dinner afterwards. Frida notices that Heinz is a little sad but decides not to ask about it in the midst of so many people.

The celebrations have finished, and the groom carries his beloved bride home in his arms.

"Are you sure you can carry me? It's two kilometers to our house," Frida says, smiling.

"I can, and I want you to get home rested up," Heinz confirms.

"But if I'm rested and you're not, what fun is that?" Frida asks smiling.

"You'll be on top," Heinz replies, provoking Frida.

"With pleasure," she states, chuckling. "But why are you sad?" Frida inquires, ruffling his hair.

"I'm happy. I'm not sad," Heinz says, trying to change his face.

"I know that you're not. I can see that. Didn't you want to marry me?" Frida asks.

"Yes, I did, and I still want to be your husband… It's just …" Heinz pauses. "… I'd like my mother to have seen you in your bridal gown," he adds.

"I thought your parents were dead. You never talk about them," Frida says.

"My father is. He died from war wounds," Heinz states.

"Your father was in the army, too?" Frida asks.

"I'm the third generation of the Fritz family in the German army," he replies proudly.

"What was your father's name?" she asks.

"Franz, and my mother's Eileen. My father adored that name," Heinz recalls.

"Why didn't your mother come?" Frida inquires. "Was she against our marriage?"

"My uncle couldn't find her," he said, worried, putting Frida down so he could open the door.

"She wasn't at your home?" Frida asks,

"My uncle tried. She's not in Munich," Heinz responds, laying Frida on the bed.

"Don't you want to look for her?" Frida queries.

"I think I know where she is. And it may be better for no one to find her. That way, she'll be safe," Heinz replies.

"But, what if she's not well? Doesn't that worry you?"

"My mother's courageous. She knows how to fight. My father taught her and me," Heinz says. "I'm going to do the same thing for you," he adds.

"I don't want to fight. I'm peaceful. I'd rather talk. My father always kept me away from things related to war," Frida replies.

"Col. Myer was a great officer. I respect his memory, but his being a high ranking officer and keeping war distant from you was a grave mistake," Heinz adds.

"Why?" Frida inquires.

"Because if someone comes here to do you harm someday and I'm not nearby, I'd never forgive myself for not having taught you to defend yourself. It's my duty to teach you," Heinz says.

"My father always protected me as best he could. He took me out of school and had me taught at home when they threatened him. He then bought a house far from the city and my mum and I almost never went out if he wasn't close by. He always chose to protect us instead of making us fight," Frida pauses. "And I heard him say that only his hands should be covered in blood. Was he wrong?" she asks, pensive.

"I don't know, Frida. That's a hard question." Heinz pauses. "On one hand, I understand that the colonel loved you a lot and wanted to hide the hard life of being a soldier from you. On the other, I disagree with limiting you to eternal confinement. You've grown up without knowing how to live. When you entered the real world, you were very lost, and I imagine that you've suffered a lot," Heinz says.

"My parents came to regret raising me like that. I remember a conversation I had with them; both were desperate, trying to teach me to come out of my shell. It was difficult, but I'm more or less okay," Frida confirms.

"And I want you to continue being okay at my side and in my absence. I'm going to teach you to fight because I don't want you to be a prisoner. You're my lovely butterfly and need to fly. If I have to teach you to fight so you can continue flying, then I will," Heinz says.

The next morning, he set up a sandbag in the back yard and got a pistol.

"Come here, Frida. I'm going to teach you how to shoot," Heinz states.

"When you said you were going to teach me to fight, I thought you were going to teach me to fight physically, not with guns," she says.

"During a war, they're not going to physically fight a woman. They'll shoot her, because it's quick and simple," Heinz responds.

She hesitates, but understands that, for him, this is very important.

Heinz teachers Frida how to handle a pistol, how to load it, and how to take the safety off, among other details he considered important.

"Now, keep your grip firm and aim. Aiming is more important than firing," Heinz says. "You need to practice aiming, since if you shoot and miss, you become your enemy's target, understand? You have to hit him first," Heinz adds.

Frida spends the day practicing and discovers that shooting isn't that simple.

After a week of intensive training, she hits the target with ease for the very first time.

"I did it!" Frida exclaims in German.

"Congratulations! I'm proud of you!" Heinz replies. "Who knows? Maybe with practice you'll get supper right, too," Heinz adds, chuckling.

"You know how to cook. I give up. I'm really bad. There's no helping me," Frida says.

Heinz steps close to her and whispers in her ear, in English, "You've learned to speak German and learned to shoot. There's nothing that you can't do on your own when you practice," Heinz smiles and kisses her.

Frida feels challenged by Heinz's comment and visits Nina in the early afternoon.

"Will you teach me to cook?" Frida pleads.

"What do you mean, my dear? To cook?" Nina questions.

"Do you know how?" Frida asks.

"Of course, I do, but I thought you did, too. Who cooks for you?" Nina asks.

"Sometimes I try, but Heinz cooks most of the time," she confesses, embarrassed.

"I thought your mother'd taught you," Heinz's aunt says.

"My mother didn't cook," Frida responds.

"You must have been rich, then," states Heinz's aunt.

"Yes, we were," Frida replies, remembering her parents.

"What do you want to learn?" Nina asks.

"Teach me something easy that I can make for supper tonight.," Frida pleads.

"I've got a cookbook I used when I got married. You should be able to learn a lot from it," she says, leading them to the library.

"Do you think I can learn how to cook by reading a book?" inquires Frida.

"You can learn a lot reading a good book. I know you like to read," Nina responds.

Frida begins to smile, remembering that she's learned a large part of her German from books.

Nina hands her the book and provides her with some ingredients so Frida can cook supper.

When she returns home, she spends the rest of the afternoon cooking, faithfully following the instructions in the book.

Arriving home after his afternoon duties, Heinz enters the house and smells the delightful aroma of a pie.

"Did you make the pie by yourself?" Heinz inquires surprised.

"I did... You aunt gave me this book and I made the pie. You came home late today. I think it's gotten cold," Frida replies, looking at the clock.

"You can heat it up again. Put it back in the oven," he says, kissing her.

Heinz leaves the kitchen and takes a shower. Frida surprises him and enters the shower stall, too.

They spend some time in the shower, until he smells something strange.

"Frida, did you put the pie back in the oven?" Heinz asks.

"Yes, that's what you told me to do, isn't it?" Frida responds.

"You put the pie in the oven and came after me?" Heinz quizzes, running, wrapping himself in a towel.

Frida, distressed, does the same and runs to the kitchen.

"My pie!" Frida exclaims, crying.

"You know something, dear... I don't care about cooking. Let me do it," Heinz says, smiling, taking the burnt pie from the oven.

"Good… I've officially done something worse than the cake," she declares, now smiling.

"I don't think we can possibly eat this, so I agree," Heinz replies, tossing the pie in the trash.

# Chapter XVII

Heinz wakes up rather pensive that weekend. Concerned, Frida asks, "Is anything wrong. You were quiet all through breakfast."

"We're going to practice shooting some more," Heinz says.

They go to the back yard and Frida hits the target three times in a row.

"I'm proud of you, Frida. Will you promise me that you'll keep on practicing" Heinz ask, holding her hand.

"What's happening, Heinz?" Frida asks, worried.

"I'm going to have to leave for a couple of months. I have an important mission," Heinz says, entering the house.

"What do you mean, a couple of months? What mission? You can't leave me alone," she pleads, distressed.

"I have to go, Frida. The war is much larger than you think. I'll go to Italy to help with intelligence for our troops," Heinz responds.

"But why you? Why don't you send someone? Aren't you a sergeant?" Frida asks.

"I'll be going with my team. I need to go. My general insists that I'm the best on the team and I have to go. If I don't go, they'll shoot me, and you'd be next," Heinz explains.

"But why did you have to be so good?" Frida asks.

"I don't think I'm the best, but my general insists that I am," Heinz says, smiling.

He walks to the bookshelf, grabs a book and leafs through it until an envelope falls out onto the floor.

"What's that? A letter?" Frida asks.

"Yes, it is. I received it a few months before I met you," Heinz responds, sitting down and opening the envelope.

"What is it?" Frida enquired, distressed.

"It's a letter from my mother," he pauses and then continues. "She wrote me that she'd bought a farm in a city called Luckenwalde, near Berlin. It's about 50 kilometers from Berlin. She said she was happy planting cotton," Heinz says, handing the letter to Frida.

"So, you know where your mother is?" Frida asks.

"God willing, she's at the address in the letter." Heinz takes a sheet of paper and begins to write.

"What are you doing? Say something," Frida pleads, in aguish.

"Give me a couple of minutes and I will," says Heinz, who continues writing.

A few minutes later, he pauses, folds the paper, puts it in an envelope, and seals it shut.

"I'll write my mother's name and address here on the envelope," Heinz explains.

"Are you going to send your mother a letter?" Frida inquires.

"Pay attention, Frida. I'm going to tell you something and I want you to memorize everything I say without question, please," Heinz says, taking Frida's hand and placing the letter in it. "Tomorrow, I'm leaving for Italy. I don't know when I'll be back, but I won't write you to tell you when, since it's important for your safety that the enemy not know I have a family." Heinz sits next to Frida. "If Germany wins the war, you'll know, because it'll be on the radio and the base will really celebrate. As soon as we win, I'll return to get you. If Germany loses, it won't take long for them to invade this base. If you know in advance, flee to my mother's house and I'll find you there. Do you understand?"

"Your mother doesn't know me," Frida says, confused and anguished.

"I know, which is the reason for the letter. Give it to her. She knows me, knows that I'd never give her location away," Heinz replies. "Give it to her personally. Don't let this letter fall into anyone else's hands."

"But why do you have to go? Why this stupid war?" Frida says, crying.

"Frida, you'll have to be strong now. Our family depends on this," Heinz replies, hugging her. "Keep practicing. Shooting is important. I've asked my uncle to give you ammunition and sandbags every week."

"It's one thing to shoot at a sandbag, another to shoot a person," Frida says, crying. "I won't be able to."

"I know, Frida. It's hard. Think about me, think about the family we want to build and defend that family, just like I'll be doing in Italy," Heinz says.

Frida cries compulsively.

"I know it's going to be hard. For me, too. But think about this: the soldier who wants to hurt you is only trying to defend his family, just like you're defending yours. It's a question of will. Whoever has the most will and is better trained wins, and I know you'll be able to win," Heinz says, kissing Frida's head, which is in his lap.

"You'll come home, won't you?" Frida asks.

"Yes, I will," he answers firmly. "Pay attention. I built a closet in the corner of the living room. It has a door with several holes and is camouflaged. If the light is turned off, it's hard to see it. I built a small shelf in the back, where there's a loaded pistol. Clean that pistol every month and reload it like I taught you. It's important for you to do this, or the gun will jam and, then it won't work if you need it. Never forget to return the gun to its hiding place loaded," Heinz says.

"How will I know when to hide" Frida asks.

"If you hear a lot of shouting, for whatever reason, hide and wait. Don't come out until the shouting is over, understand?" Heinz orients her.

"I understand, but what if they find me?" Frida questions.

"Use the gun. Don't think about it, don't hesitate, since they won't hesitate either. Have you got that?" Heinz asks, looking Frida in the eyes.

"I can't do it," Frida claims, crying.

"Yes, you can. I'll be back and hope you can... for me, or at least try with your head held high," he says.

She responds by shaking her head yes while Heinz begins to fix his backpack.

The next morning, before dawn, he says goodbye to Frida.

"Remember what I said. Go to my mother's if you need to. I'll be back," Heinz says before kissing her.

"You'd better return or I'll go there looking for you."

"This break will be good for us. Who knows? Maybe you'll learn to cook, or you'll die of hunger," Heinz says, grinning.

"I love you, you idiot!" Frida confirms.

They kiss and Heinz leaves in his vehicle.

# Chapter XVIII

Frida doesn't want to do anything all morning. She just sits on the sofa and thinks about everything Heinz told her the day before. The more she thought, the lonelier she realized she was.

"I'm going to be alone in this world. Dad, I now know why you worried so much about me," Frida says, crying and remembering her last conversations with her parent.

Without realizing it, she goes into a deep depression and doesn't want to do anything. She just looks at the ceiling of her house and a photo she'd taken with Heinz on their wedding day.

The hours go by quickly and, at five in the evening, she hears someone knocking at the door. Desperate and afraid, she runs to the closet Heinz made and checks where the pistol is. Before she can touch the weapon, she hears a familiar voice.

"Frida, dear, are you okay?"

It was Nina. Frida runs to the door and opens it.

"Are you all right?" Nina asks again. "My husband told me Heinz had to leave. I imagined that you needed a friendly shoulder," she adds, hugging Frida, who begins to cry.

"I'm going to lose him," she exclaims in German.

"Don't be silly, dear. Fritz's family has a strong reputation in the German army for courage and integrity. My husband's proud of his nephew. You should have faith in him," Nina says, trying to calm Frida.

"I was afraid of losing my father the first time he left home and I did lose him. Now, the same thing's going to happen to Heinz," Frida says, sitting on the couch.

"Your father was killed in a bombing raid, right?" Nina asks. Frida shakes her head yes. "It wasn't because of your father's abilities. It was fate," she completes.

"I know, but I ended up losing both him and my mother," Frida responds. "The same fate could happen to Heinz, too," she says.

"Yes, that's true... We'll pray every day. That's all we can do," Nina suggests.

Frida remains quiet for a few seconds and Nina goes to the kitchen.

"What have you eaten today?" she asks, realizing the kitchen was completely clean.

"I just had breakfast with Heinz, before he left," Frida replies.

"That was over twelve hours ago. You need to eat," Nina says, looking for something in the kitchen.

"I don't want to eat anything," Frida states.

"You'll get sick. Heinz will get desperate, wherever he is... Come on, let's cook something together," Nina says, pulling Frida from the couch.

Frida hesitates, but perceiving Nina's kindness and persistence, she stands up.

"Let's go. I'm going to teach you to cook using the book I gave you. When Heinz returns, you'll be a master chef," she states.

"I don't think I was born to cook. There's a force in nature that keeps me from learning," Frida replies, who smiles briefly, remembering all the meals she's made for Heinz.

"Don't be foolish. All you need is practice... Come over every morning and we'll fix lunch together, okay?", Nina asks.

Frida can't refuse the friendly offer from her husband's aunt and promises to visit her the following morning.

Time passes and, as promised, every morning, Frida visited and learned a little more about how to cook for herself. In the afternoons, Frida divided her time between target practice and learning more of her husband's language.

Twenty days had gone by since Heinz's departure, and she kept up the same routine. That morning, however, Frida didn't feel well and sent a note to Nina saying she wouldn't be there because she didn't feel well. Three days had passed by, and the notes continued reaching Heinz's aunt, who began to worry.

On the fourth day that a note arrives, Nina decides to visit Frida. She then knocks on the door of Frida's house, who doesn't answer it quickly.

"Frida, it's me. Open the door," she says, concerned.

Frida finally appears and opens the door. Her face is pale, and she can barely stand on her feet by herself.

"My God, Frida, what's happened?" Nina asks, helping her to the sofa.

"I'm weak and feel nauseous. Nothing stays down," she replies with difficulty.

Nina realizes the situation is serious and asks for help getting Frida to her house.

A doctor is quickly called, and Heinz's aunt and uncle are anxious to hear what the doctor has to say.

Two hours later, the doctor returns from the room where Frida was.

"What is it, doctor? Is it serious?" Heinz's aunt asks anxiously.

"She'll be fine, but she needs bedrest and mustn't engage in physical activity, so she doesn't hemorrhage again," the doctor replies.

"She was hemorrhaging?" Claus asks.

"Yes, and there was a lot of blood. She almost lost the baby," the doctor confirms, giving them some medication.

"Baby? What is the medication for?" Nina asks, distressed.

"Yes, she's almost three months pregnant. The medicine is to help stop her hemorrhaging and to keep her strong," the doctor adds.

"Did she know she was pregnant?" asks Claus.

"No, she didn't. When I told her, she fainted. Her menstrual cycle was normal, which is why she almost miscarried," the doctor continues. "She needs a lot of bedrest," the doctors say and then quickly leaves the house.

Heinz's aunt and uncle run to Frida's room, where she is lying down, crying.

"Congratulations!" Claus exclaims.

"I'm going to be a single mother," she says, sobbing.

"That's foolish, Frida. Heinz will be home soon! You're married and pregnant. There's nothing wrong with that," Nina, asserts, sitting next to Frida.

"I don't know what I'm going to do without Heinz… I can barely take care of myself," Frida says, continuing to cry.

"We're family. You'll stay here with us in our home until the doctor releases you from bedrest. I'm going to help you," Claus says, holding her hand.

"Maybe it'd be better to write Heinz and let him know," Frida suggests.

"There is no way I'll let you send that letter," Claus says. "He already has more than enough to worry about. We'll just distract him and there's nothing he can do anyway. It could be bad for him, or even fatal, if he can't concentrate," he adds.

"Heinz told me not to write him, so the enemy shouldn't discover that he has a family," Frida remembers.

"He's right. Respect what he asked you," Claus adds.

The medication the doctor had given her is now beginning to take effect, so she calms down and fall sleep. Heinz's aunt and uncle let her rest.

Two months later Frida has feeling stronger and able to do her routine tasks.

"I need to go home," Frida tells Heinz's aunt.

"No way! Look at that belly! You need help," Nina replies.

"My dear, if you feel well enough to go home, you know that you've also got a place here," Claus says, taking her hand.

"She can't go. You can't let her!" Nina angrily exclaims.

"Don't worry, my dear wife. You've been marvelous company and she will miss you," Claus calmly adds.

"I love both of you as my second parents, but I need to learn to do things by myself. I have a child to take care of," Frida says, rubbing her belly.

Upon taking her leave of Heinz's aunt and uncle and of their house, Frida slowly walks home and, once again, feels alone. The baby lightly kicks her belly, which makes her place her hand on it.

"I know, dear, Mommy knows you're there," Frida says, smiling.

# Chapter XIX

Frida was in her eighth month of pregnancy and news about the war was the main topic of conversation on the base, now full of only women and children; the remaining soldiers were there to defend the base.

"I think we'll have one more year of war!" exclaims Frida's neighbor at the fence.

Frida, pinning clothes on the line, didn't feel like talking so she didn't reply to her neighbor, who stayed at the fence.

"Your belly is really big! How long will it be?" she asks, trying to continue the conversation.

"About four weeks, more or less," Frida replies, without looking at her neighbor.

"You talk funny... Are you a foreigner?" the neighbor queries, curious.

Frida feels a cold chill and drops her basket of clothes unintentionally.

"Are you all right?" the woman asks.

"Yes, I just felt dizzy. I think I've been out in the sun too long," Frida apologizes.

"You spend your mornings shooting at that sandbag. You must be exhausted," the neighbor continues.

"Yes, I am. I think I'm going to lie down. Excuse me," Frida says, entering her house.

"My God, does she know?" Frida asks herself, frightened.

To protect herself, she decides to go out as little as possible, and to stay quiet most of the time.

Just one week before she was due, she accepted Claus and Nina's invitation and returns to live with them temporarily.

"Thanks!" Frida proclaims. "I can't get around very well. My legs and back hurt," she says, placing her hands where it hurt.

"That's normal, dear. This baby will come soon," Nina responds, rather excited about Frida's return.

"Excuse me for asking, but do you have children? We've never talked about that," Frida asks very delicately.

"No, I can't have children," Nina replies sadly.

"I'm sorry. I didn't mean to upset you," Frida says, repentant.

"Don't worry about it. You had no way of knowing," she pauses, "but I have my nephews and nieces," she finishes, smiling.

"Of course!" Frida smiles.

Three days after arriving at the big house, she feels her first contractions while going to the living room.

"Ouch! Call a doctor!" she yells, kneeling on the floor.

Nina quickly calls while Claus carries Frida to her room.

She spends the day in labor and, in the early evening, the cry of a baby echoes throughout the house.

"It's a boy, Frida! He's lovely!" Nina exclaims, with the child in her arms. She takes the baby to his mother, who can't hold him because she was very weak.

"It's okay, dear. Rest. I'll look after him," Nina says.

As soon as Frida was clean and drifting off, Claus asks to enter the room and see the child. They promptly let him in.

"He's so gorgeous!" Claus exclaims with the child in his arms. "Have you picked a name for him?" he asks.

"Franz. We'll call him Franz!" Frida replies, with her vision very blurred.

"That was the name of Heinz's father," Claus says.

"Yes, it was," Frida confirms, looking at no one.

"My sister would be happy if she were here," Claus comments.

"I think Heinz will like it," Frida says. She then falls asleep because she was so tired.

They let her rest and take little Franz with them.

During Franz's first month of life, Nina doesn't let Frida live alone and spends much of her day helping take care of Franz.

The day finally arrives when Frida can return home.

"Franz, let's go to our house to wait for Dad," she says, kissing the child.

Upon reaching her destination, she notices that one of the rooms had been totally redecorated. There was a crib, a stroller, and closet full of baby clothes and toys. Frida places Franz in the crib and notices a note on the pillow.

"This is our present for our great nephew. Welcome home, Franz!"

Frida cries when she reads the note because she'd been very worried about finding the money to buy clothes for her son. She'd even learned how to fix her own clothes since she didn't receive much money from Heinz's salary and was saving up in case she needed to flee.

The days went by and Frida neighbors visited her often, helping her by donating their children's old clothes and toys. Because of this, little Franz was a rich and happy child.

When he began to crawl, she realized Franz would begin talking soon. It would be important for him to learn both English and German in the future, so Frida talked to him in both, and he quickly learned some words in the two languages.

Little Franz was pure charisma. He was one of the prettiest babies on the base and attracted attention from everyone because of his angelic smile.

His green eyes and blond hair were like Heinz's, which sometimes affected Frida. She always cried when she remembered her husband.

When Franz's first birthday arrived, Frida realized that she'd hadn't heard anything from Heinz in more than a year.

Their son learned to walk easily and was even constructing sentences in German and English.

"Remember, little man, never speak English with anyone but me," Frida says.

"Mommy, where's Daddy?" Franz askes, with a photo of Heinz in his hands.

"He's working, son. He'll be back some day," Frida replies, trying to hold back her tears.

Franz was enrolled in a small school on the base, which helped him learn German more quickly.

At three years of age, Franz spoke both languages fluently and perfectly. He even frequently helped correct his mother's accent.

"Mommy, five kids were crying at school today," Franz says, sadly.

"What happened, son? Did they fall?" Frida asks, placing him on her lap.

"No, Mommy. Their daddies died. It was in the paper," Franz says.

"In the paper?" Frida asks, curious.

"Yes, in the paper… Mommy, is Daddy dead?" Franz wonders, without really understanding what that meant.

"I…. I," Frida stammered nervously.

Frida runs to the window and realizes that there was no movement, so she decides to go out. She finds a neighbor and asks, "Has another casualty list arrived?"

"Yes, I just saw it. My husband isn't on it, thank God!" her neighbor says.

"My God, the lists are arriving quicker and quicker now," Frida says, anxiously.

She returns home, picks up Franz, and runs to the center of the base, where the lists were posted. Near the lists, she could identify the screams of pain and happiness that mixed together in the air.

"Is Daddy there, Mommy?" Franz asks.

Frida reads as fast as she can, three times, until she sighs, relieved.

"No, son. Your daddy's not on the list."

The next day, another list arrives, and Frida begins to understand that something's wrong. She runs to Claus's house.

"Are we losing the war?" Frida queries anxiously.

"We're suffering many losses, but no one has told me whether we're winning or losing," Claus pauses. "I've already checked today's list. Heinz isn't on it."

"And you, do you personally think we're losing?" Frida asks, nervously.

"I think it'll be better if you don't take Franz to school. Stay at home more," Claus replies, concerned.

Frida returns home and realizes that many of her neighbors no longer lived there because the heads of their families had died. She decides then to start arranging her things.

"Are we going to take a trip, Mommy?" Franz asks.

"Yes, we are, dear. Speak to Mommy only in German from now on, okay?" Frida responds, uneasily.

"But we'll get back before Daddy, won't we?" he asks, packing his toys.

Frida remembers that Heinz had told her to stay there and to only leave if the war ended and Germany lost.

She then calms down, takes a seat, and looks at her son.

"We're going to wait for Daddy. Then we'll take a trip."

Franz kisses his mother and begins to play with his car.

# Chapter XX

A week later, Frida notices that the radio no longer works, and the power was going out more frequently.

She then decides that the time to leave has finally come and packs their things.

"Tomorrow morning, we're leaving, son," Frida says, placing all the money she'd saved in a small purse.

"We're not going to wait for Daddy anymore?" Franz asks.

"No, he'll meet us there," Frida replies, hanging her purse by the front door.

Frida lays Franz down to sleep and extinguishes the fire in the hearth, goes to the kitchen to drink a glass of milk. She then closes the house's backdoor. When she goes to close the front door, she notices unusual movement on the base.

Frida quickly turns off the house's lights and soon begins to hear shouts and shooting. She grabs her small purse and runs to Franz's room. Frightened by the noise, he was crying.

"Son, do you remember what Mommy told you about bad men and our hidey-hole?" Frida asks, putting her son on her lap.

Franz shakes his head yes and stops crying.

"We're going to the hidey-hole," Frida says, running to the closet.

Before closing the door, she takes the gun and all the ammunition her bag can hold.

Franz stays quiet and frightened, waiting for his mother to return. Frida reappears, enters the closet, closes the door, and places her son behind her.

The noise and shouting increased, and Franz was trembling, but his mother had never felt as strong in her life. She was looking through the hole in the closet and remembered in detail all of the instructions Heinz had given her for that moment.

The sound of shooting approached her door, and with one of her hands, she covered Franz's mouth, who was so frightened he was barely breathing.

"Someone's still living here," a soldier said in English.

"Are you sure?" asks the other soldier, from outside the house.

"The fireplace's still warm," he states, causing the other soldier to come inside.

Both of them search the house, and Frida knew that it would be a question of minutes before they found her.

"Look, it's a sergeant's house," said one of the soldiers, looking at the photo of Heinz in uniform on the table.

Frida felt a chill, since she knew that they'd soon find her. "Don't hesitate, because they won't. It's a question of will," she heard Heinz's voice in her head. All her life, her parents, Heinz, all of those moments and decisions had led to that situation. "But Franz, he's never had a choice," Frida thinks. "I need to get him out of here… He has the right to choose. I'm going to protect him, so he can choose his future." Frida now grips the pistol more tightly and whispers in her son's ear, "Don't move, don't say anything, cover your ears, and close your eyes."'

Franz obeys his mother, covers his ears, and closes his eyes.

"Look at the sergeant's wife. She's a beauty," say a soldier, chuckling, pointing at the Frida's wedding picture.

"Come on, cutie pie, we want to have some fun. We know you're here," shouts one of the soldiers, laughing.

From their accents, Frida realizes that one of the soldiers is English and the other's American. She waits a little longer and makes sure there are only two soldiers in her house.

"Look, there's a closet!" one of the soldiers points out.

The other soldier who was closer opens the closet door. Frida shoots him in the head without hesitating. She then crouches in front of her son. The soldier falls to the ground, freeing her field of vision. She can see that the second soldier is ready to fire. Frida is quicker, also hitting him in the head.

She takes Franz's hands from his ears and tells him, "Don't open your eyes. Stay here. Mommy will be right back."

Frida, crouching, runs to the window and checks if there are more soldiers coming in their direction, but sees none nearby. She returns to Franz.

"Stay there a little longer, with your eyes closed."

She takes a backpack that she'd already prepared and returns to the closet where her son still had his eyes closed. Frida reloads the pistol, takes her small purse and hugs Franz.

"Don't look, son!", she says, holding him in her arms.

Frida goes to the back of the house and jumps over the small fence in the yard. She then picks up Franz, who was waiting for her on the other side. The noise and shouting continue. She sees a tall tree and helps her son climb it. The darkness above will hide them, and she can wait until the shouting dies down.

Two hours later, the shouting has calmed down. Frida decides to climb down. Franz is still quiet and frightened, but he follows his mother without hesitation.

Both of them walk, crouching in the dark. That way, they skirt around some drunken soldiers who are celebrating their victory.

Frida remembers there's only one entrance and exit to the base. She's walking toward it when Franz stops.

"Come on, son, we need to go!" Frida says, pulling him.

"And Uncle?" Franz asks, referring to Claus.

Frida knew the first place to be attacked would be the large house, just like what had happened at the British base. She was sure there was little probability that Heinz's aunt and uncle were still alive. But she knew that Franz really liked them, because they treated him like a grandson.

"They left earlier. We'll meet them later," Frida lied with a heavy heart.

They both approach the area of the base entrance and, as she'd feared, it was heavily guarded by enemy soldiers.

Frida hides behind a tree and observes the entrance. All the soldiers were celebrating, but there were too many for her to slip by without being noticed, so Frida decides to try a risky idea.

She sees one of the soldiers move away from the group to relieve himself on one of the trees. The celebration was extremely noisy, and Frida imagined the group wouldn't hear the sound of a shot.

Frida aims like she's never had before. She has only one chance. Franz, seeing that his mother was going to fire again, covers his ears and eyes. Frida then shoots, hitting the soldier in the forehead. He falls without reacting.

The sound of the shot did not, in fact, stop the group's commemoration. They continue drinking and singing.

Frida places her backpack and purse in the tree and makes Franz wait for her. She then runs to the soldier, takes his clothes and dresses as a soldier. She carefully tucks her hair into the soldier's helmet and, with great effort, drags his body behind the tree.

Frida, duly dressed, enters the group of soldiers who, drunk, don't notice her arrival. She desperately looks for a trunk to hid Franz in. Since she can't find a trunk, she takes a sleeping bag and returns to the tree, where Franz, still frightened, has his eyes closed.

"Son, Mommy's going to put you in this sleeping bag. Don't make any noise until I take you out."

Frida realizes that she won't be able to carry everything she'd like to, so she places Franz, her purse, a dress and a pair of shoes in the sleeping bag. Before closing it, she gives her son a kiss and prays.

After praying, she holds the sack and tries to hide what's in it as best she can.

She passes the first group of soldiers and, when reaching the second, one of the soldiers speaks to her in English.

"Are you tired?" asks the soldier

"I'm just going to put the sack up, and I'll be right back," she says, deepening her voice.

The soldier was extremely drunk and barely pays any attention to her. She keeps on walking.

Far from the soldiers, Frida enters the forest and hides near the road, where she takes Franz from the sleeping bag.

It was very cold, and she realized that the soldier's clothing was warmer than her dress. She also notices that Franz is trembling from the cold and puts him back in the sleeping bag, leaving his head sticking out. It was impossible to sleep in that cold, so Frida decides to continue walking, next to the highway, to stay warm until sunrise. Moving about, she kept her blood circulating and felt less cold.

After walking for an hour, Frida was exhausted. She puts Franz on the ground and sits down for a few minutes.

"You fit in here, Mommy!" Franz says, lifting the sleeping bag up.

Frida puts her dress, shoes, and purse next to her gun and lies down with Franz in the sleeping bag. Fatigue makes both of them fall to sleep quickly.

The sun rises and, luckily for them, it is less cold.

"Mommy, wake up!" Franz says, kissing her face.

Frida wakes up startled, but quickly realizes it's her son.

"What is it, son? Are you all right?" she asks, concerned.

"I'm hungry, Mommy!" he replies, rubbing his stomach.

Frida remembers they'd left the food in the backpack they'd abandoned.

"Mommy doesn't have any food right now, son. We need to wait a little," she says, as she begins to remove the soldier's clothes to put her dress on.

After walking for an hour, her son is exhausted, and Frida needs to carry him. Going a little further, she notices a farm on the other side of the highway. Because she was tired and hungry, she decides to try to talk to the farm's owner.

She approaches the house in the center of the farm and a man points a weapon at her. She immediately stops.

"Please don't shoot. My son and I are hungry. Can you help us? I have money," Frida says desperately in German.

A woman appears from inside the house and lowers her husband's weapon. He irritatedly shouts at her, "Can't you see that she's armed?"

"If you wish, you can come here and take my gun. What I want more than anything is to be rid of it!" Frida says, tossing the gun in front of her.

"Pick up your gun, take the bullets out of it and throw it to me," the man orders, still pointing his at Frida.

She lets Franz's hand go and does what the man orders.

"Please, ma'am, help me! My son's hungry. I can pay," Frida begs, desperately.

The older man retrieves her gun from the ground and lets her enter.

"Don't pay any attention to my husband. He's just trying to protect me. Come on inside. You must be freezing," says the woman.

Frida smiles and enters the house. The woman then offers both of them bread and milk.

"What's the little one's name?" she asks.

"I'm Franz. Thank you for the milk," Franz replies, hungrily devouring the milk.

"What are you doing with a child out on this road?" the man asks.

"I lived at the military base near here. We had to flee," Frida replies.

"Was your husband a soldier?" the man asks.

"He isn't dead, or at least I don't think he is," Frida pauses. "Yes, he was, or still is, a sergeant."

"What's your name, dear?" the woman asks.

"Frida, thank you very much. What should I call you?" she asks.

"I'm Ruth and that's Peter, my husband," the woman replies.

"Those damned Americans think they own the world now," Peter complains.

"Is the war over? Do you know anything?" Frida questions.

"The Russians and Americans have begun attacking Berlin, those bastards!" Peter says.

"And what about Italy, do you know anything?" Frida asks, anguished.

"Mussolini surrendered, that weakling!" Peter replies.

"Ignore my husband. He's very passionate," Ruth says, giving Franz more milk.

"I didn't go fight because I have a bad leg," Peter states, sitting next to Franz. "Your father's a hero, little one."

"I know," Franz responds.

"Your son's very handsome," Ruth says.

'I know," Franz replies, which makes everyone laugh.

Frida takes some money from her purse and gives it to Ruth, who gives it back.

"Keep it, dear. You'll need it," she says.

"Where are you going?" Peter asks.

"I need to catch a train," Frida responds. "Which way is the station?"

"The closest station is about ten kilometers from here," Peter says. "It's too far to walk."

"I need to try," Frida says.

"I'll take you in my car," the man says, looking at Franz. "I can't let this boy freeze."

"I'll be eternally grateful," Frida responds, with tears in her eyes.

"But I can only take you tomorrow, when I go downtown," Peter adds.

"You can sleep in our son's room. He doesn't live here anymore," Ruth says.

"I'll never be able to repay such kindness," Frida asserts.

Franz is all joy. He plays and cheers everyone in the house up with his innocence and happiness.

"Look, Mommy. That grandpa gave me this!" Franz says, showing a top.

"Asks Grandpa to teach you how to play with it!" she replies, smiling.

To repay the favor, Frida offers to help with the housework and the day goes by peacefully for Frida and Franz.

# Chapter XXI

The next morning, Frida gets up early and fixes the couple breakfast.

"Thank you, Frida!" Ruth says.

When Peter finishes eating, she takes the sleeping bag and her purse.

"Are you going to keep on carrying that bag?" Ruth asks.

"Yes, I couldn't bring Franz's jacket, so I'm using the bag to carry him," Frida responds.

Ruth leaves for a moment and returns with some clothes.

"I didn't have time to wash these coats, but I think they'll help you," Ruth pauses and shows one of the pieces. "I kept some of my son's clothes from when he was little. I think this will fit him!" she says, looking at Franz. "and this is my coat. Put it on to see if it fits you."

Frida puts one coat on Franz and the other on herself.

"They're perfect! Thank you so much, Ruth!", she responds, touched.

Frida and Franz say goodbye to Ruth and get into the car with Peter.

"Excuse me being so forward, but where are you planning to take the child?" Peter asks.

"I'm going to Berlin," Frida says.

"Berlin? Now?" Peter questions.

Frida nods yes with her head.

"That's insane," Peter says, agitated. "Nobody's entering or leaving Berlin! The stations are being monitored by American troops and the Russian are going to invade any day now. Not even Hitler's in Berlin at this point! What are you going to do with a child there?" Peter adds.

"I'm not going to stay in Berlin. I'm going to a city nearby. I promised my husband I'd wait for him there," Frida replies.

"You know your husband's probably..." Peter looks at Franz, who is sleeping. "You know your husband must be dead. Don't risk your child's life," Peter says in a lower voice.

"I promised that I'd try, and I will, but I thank you for your concern," Frida responds gently.

Peter leaves them at the station and, with a heavy heart, continues his trip.

Frida buys two tickets to Berlin and, once more, is warned by the clerk who doesn't believe she'll get past the platform.

The trip is slow because of bombing in the region. Trains have to stop and wait for authorization to continue. The train arrives in Berlin late in the afternoon. Few people risk getting off, and Frida, determined, whispers in Franz's ear, "Dear, if Mommy speaks English, you speak in English, but if Mommy speaks German, don't speak English, okay?"

Franz shows that he's understood, and Frida enters a small line forming in front of a barrier manned by soldiers. She makes sure she's at the end of the line and, nervous, thinks about what to say.

She notices that few people are let through. Most are turned back. Worried, but with a plan in mind, Frida is next.

"What are you doing in Berlin?" a soldier in an American uniform asks in German.

"Would you please repeat the question in English?" Frida asks.

"What's a Brit doing in Berlin? Especially these days?" the soldier ask, noticing her accent.

"I came to visit my husband. He's with the army," Frida responds, flipping her hair and looking at the soldier with a charming smile.

"Are you crazy or stupid? Your husband isn't on vacation in Berlin. Didn't you know that?" the soldier asks angrily. "And you're travelling with a child," he adds, pointing at Franz.

"I haven't seen my husband in a year and I don't know if he's dead or alive. I needed to come. I have to try," Frida says, taking out a handkerchief, drying a false tear.

"I miss Daddy!" Franz exclaims in English.

"I doubt you'll find your husband, and if I were you, I'd give you a whipping if you found me," the soldier replies.

"Are you married?" Frida asks, looking the soldier directly in the eyes.

"No, I'm not," he answers.

"What a waste. You must be very popular with the girls," Frida says, flirting with the soldier, who begins to smile.

"Are you planning your future in case your husband's dead?" the soldier inquires, laughing.

"I wonder if I'd have a chance with a soldier as handsome as you," Frida pauses, smiling. "I need to find my husband," she adds.

"Okay, lady. I'll let you by," says the soldier, opening the gate.

When Frida goes through, the soldier takes her arm and whispers in her ear, "If you don't find him, come back to this station and I'll take care of your missing him," the soldier says, kissing her face. She smiles.

"Of course, I'll come back," Frida states, winking at the soldier.

Frida's attitude leaves her angry with herself, even though she needed to enter Berlin and the plan had worked.

Going into the train station, she perceives the chaos in Berlin: debris all over and outside the station, people running and soldiers everywhere.

Frida spots a mural with a large map of Berlin and nearby cities. She begins looking for the city were Heinz's mother is. Luckenwalde is about 51 kilometers from Berlin. It would be impossible to walk to the city and trains are no longer leaving Berlin; they're just arriving.

She finds an American soldier and asks in English, "Are there buses leaving Berlin?"

"Lady, I have no idea what you're doing in Germany, but this city's at war right now. If you find any transportation, there will be soldier in it," he responds and then runs off.

The noise from shooting and bombs in the region is constant and Franz, very frightened, covers his ears and cries. Frida picks her child up, looks all around, and prays in front of the station, looking for a solution to her current problem.

In her moment of anguish, she spots a woman with a child and runs toward her.

"Please, ma'am, do you know where I can find transportation to Luckenwalde?" Frida asks in German.

"There's no public transportation now. These aren't normal times in the city," the woman replies, running to the other side of the street.

Frida follows and notices a car stop. A man helps the woman and child enter. She runs desperately with Franz in her arms and stops at the side of the car.

"Please, ma'am, give me a lift to Luckenwalde," Frida please, desperate. "I'll pay you all the money I have." Frida then takes the wad of money from her purse and shows the man, who looks at it but then ignores her and gets into the car.

"Please, ma'am, from one desperate mother to another. I need to get to Luckenwalde. It's my only chance to survive," Frida pleads, looking at the woman in the car.

"Come on, dear. Let her in. We need the money and Luckenwalde is on the way to where we're going," says the woman, holding the man's arm. He looks at Franz's desperate little eyes and replies, "Get in quickly. We need to leave Berlin before it gets dark."

Frida hastily enters the car with Franz, and the man speeds through Berlin's streets.

She realizes that it's more chaotic in the city's streets. There are bodies on the ground and debris mixing with the gray, dust-covered landscape.

As planned, the man leaves Berlin before dark and the scenery changes completely. After two hours on the road, he pulls over.

"Okay, lady, get out of the car. There's Luckenwalde," the man says nervously, pointing at the sign.

"Thank you, both of you," Frida replies, giving him all of the money she had.

The car disappears and Frida notices how dark it is on the highway. The man had left her at the city's entrance, but she couldn't see the city, so Frida begins to walk, following the signs pointing downtown.

An hour later, both were freezing and hungry, since they'd only had breakfast that morning. She finally sees the first lights in the city and notices a sign reading "Lodging" ahead.

Frida, with no money, was cold and hungry. She remembers that she was wearing a gold necklace Nina had given her on her last birthday and decides to enter the establishment.

"Good evening, ma'am. My son and I are cold, tired, and hungry. Would you be willing to accept this gold necklace in exchange for a room to sleep in and a bowl of soup?" Frida asks, placing the necklace on the table.

The woman takes the necklace and analyzes it, then looks into Frida's tear-filled eyes as she tries to warm up her child with her hands.

"Okay, follow me," the woman says, taking the key to one of the rooms.

Immediately after entering the room, Frida puts Franz on the bed and covers him up. She's afraid Franz will get sick and tries to warm him up the best she can.

A few minutes later, the woman returns with a tray.

"I brought a glass of warm milk for the boy," the woman says, placing the tray on a small table in the room.

"Thank you. God bless you," Frida returns.

She closes the door and hurries to feed her son.

"Eat, dear," Frida says.

"Where's yours, Mommy?" Franz asks.

"Mommy's going to eat this bread, dear. I'm not hungry," she lies to her child.

Franz is young, but sharp enough to catch his mother's lie, so he drinks only half the milk and eats only half the soup.

"I don't want any more, Mommy," Franz says, leaving the bowl and returning to the bed.

"Eat, Franz, you need to eat," Frida says.

"I don't want any more. My tummy hurts," Franz lies, covering himself up.

Frida eats what's left over and lies down next to him to sleep.

The following morning, they get up, use the bathroom, and go to the reception area with the room key in hand.

"Thank you, ma'am," Frida says, returning the key. "Would you tell me how to get to this address?" she asks, showing Heinz's letter, being careful to cover the name written on it.

"There's only a cotton farm there," the woman says. "Cross the street and ask the owner of that store. He frequently visits the farm," the woman adds.

Frida, anxious, leaves the lodgings and goes to the store.

"Good morning, are you the store owner?" Frida asks a gray-haired man near the cash register.

"Yes, I am," the man replies gently.

"I'm trying to find this address. The owner of the lodging house said you might be able to help me," she says, showing him the letter, once again covering up the name.

"What do you want at the farm," the man asks, frowning.

"I need to speak with the owner," Frida replies.

"If you don't know the owner, I can't help you," the man says.

"I know the owner, sort of," Frida replies.

"Tell me the owner's name and I'll help you," the man continues.

Frida hesitates, but realizes she has no choice.

"Eileen... Eileen Fritz," she says, stammering.

"How do you know that name?" the man asks.

"I need to give her a letter in person," she says.

"And who sent it?" the man questions, picking up the telephone.

Frida hesitates again, but responds, "Heinz."

The man dials a few numbers and says, "Lee, there's a woman with a child in my store. She told me your name and said that she needs to give you a letter personally, from Heinz. Do you know her?" the man asks, and then becomes silent.

Shortly thereafter, he hangs up the telephone.

"She asked you to wait here. She'll come get you," the man says.

Frida then leans against the bread counter and Franz, very hungry, looks at the bread, salivating. The man understands the child's gaze and gives him one of the pieces.

"I don't have any way to pay you," Frida says, with her eyes full of tears.

"I know," the man replies, giving a second piece of bread to her.

Franz looks at his mother, who lets him eat it. Both of them, starving, quickly devour the bread.

A few minutes later, a very beautiful and kind old woman enters the store.

"Good morning!" the woman says to the owner.

"You got here quickly," the man replies, smiling.

"Where are they?" she asks, also smiling.

The man points to Frida.

"Are you Eileen?" Frida asks, smiling.

"Let's go outside, dear. I don't want anyone to hear that name," the woman responds.

Reaching the street, the woman whispers into Frida's ear, "Please call me Lee."

Frida shakes her head yes and gives her Heinz's letter. Taking it immediately and recognizing her son's writing on the envelope, Lee begins to get emotional.

"Heinz?" Lee asks.

"Yes," Frida responds.

Lee opens the envelope and reads the letter with tears in her eyes for a few minutes. After reading it, she's too moved to speak and just kisses Frida's face, motioning for her to get into the car.

The driver opens the door for the women and, once inside the car, Lee talks to Frida.

"Should I call you Jane or Frida?"

"I haven't heard Jane for a long time. Frida will do," she replies, smiling.

"Heinz didn't mention a child in the letter," Lee says.

"When he left home, I didn't know I was pregnant," Frida pauses. "He's Heinz's son. You have my word on that."

Lee smiles, looking at Franz.

"You didn't have to tell me it's his child. I can see my little Heinz sitting on your lap," Lee replies. "What's your name, little one?"

"Franz," he answers.

"Franz, this is your grandmother. She's your father's mother, understand?" Frida asks.

Franz shakes his head yes.

"Franz was my husband's name," Lee says.

"I know. That's why I named him Franz," Frida states, kissing her son.

"How old are you, Franz?" Lee asks.

Franz holds up three fingers.

"You haven't seen my son in three years?" Lee asks, startled.

"No," responds Frida, with tears in her eyes. "I think it's been a little over three years."

"I haven't seen Heinz in over five years, almost six," Lee says. "I didn't think he'd gotten my letter."

"He did and saved it. He's still got it with him," Frida confirms. "He was very sad that you couldn't attend our wedding."

"I always figured I'd be visited someday by a woman with Heinz's child, but I never thought he'd marry her," Lee says, smiling.

"I got pregnant after the wedding," Frida returned.

"I didn't mean to offend you child. My son never was the type to commit. He must really like you," Lee says, looking at Frida.

"When I met your son, I thought he was a womanizer," she says, smiling.

"You did? Well, he must have changed quickly because, if he hadn't, you'd be sure of it," Lee replies, chuckling out loud. "That boy discovered he was handsome when he was 14 and began to cause me headaches," she adds.

"You raised him well, ma'am. He's always respected me," Frida confirms.

"You don't need to call me ma'am. Lee's fine. And I'm happy to know that my son has respected some other woman besides his mother," Lee says, chuckling. "He must have learned to respect women, because I often criticized him for not doing so."

"From my first moment with him, he was always a gentleman with me," Frida continues.

"Your power over him is impressive. I'm happy that you were able to achieve what I never could," Lee confirms.

Both smile for a few moments and then Heinz's mother asks, "Have you gotten a letter from him since he left?"

"No, he said he'd never write, so the enemy wouldn't know that I existed," Frida says.

"He learned that from his father… It's irritating, don't you think?" Lee inquires.

"I don't know how he is," she replies, looking at Franz.

"Bad news travels fast. He must be okay. He's an excellent soldier," Lee says.

"Everyone says that. And I'm alive, thanks to him," Frida adds.

"How did you learn German?" Lee asks.

"Your son taught me," Frida replies.

"My son?" she asks, startled.

"He taught me how to dance, to kiss, to date, and, above all, he taught me how to love," Frida continues, with tears in her eyes.

"I'd love to meet the Heinz you say you know," Lee confirms, smiling. "You succeeded in changing him. Love is really powerful, isn't it?"

"I can't imagine the Heinz you say you know," Frida responds, smiling. "I think he quickly realized that if he didn't change, I wouldn't go out with him."

They both laugh, and Franz sees the farm and a few cows.

"Look, Mommy, a cow!" the boy exclaims, amazed.

"It is, son!" Frida says. "He's never seen an animal close up. They weren't allowed on the base," she explains.

"You'll soon be an expert with animals, dear," Lee says.

"Mommy, look at that big house. It's bigger than Uncle Claus's!" Franz exclaims.

Frida just smiles.

"It's your new home, dear!" Lee confirms.

"Heinz's letter mentions my brother," Lee says. "How is he?"

Frida's eyes fill with tears. Lee immediately understands, and her eyes also tear up.

"Are you sure?" she asks.

"No, but I think so," Frida responds, trying to dry her eyes. "He was a very good man. He was like a second father to me. I owe him a lot," she adds.

"Yes, after Franz passed away, my brother always considered Heinz the son he never had," Lee says.

"I'm here, Grandma," Franz says, making everyone smile.

# Chapter XXII

Arriving at the house, Lee asks the driver to call the farm's employees together.

Little by little, a line forms in front of the house. Frida is still contemplating the scenery at the house and farm with Franz, who is quite excited. Lee calls the two and begins speaking with all of them.

"I want to introduce you to the newest prince on our farm." Lee motions for Franz to come near and, at his side, she continues. "This is Franz, my grandson, and that is Frida, my son's wife and my new daughter. Obey them like you obey me," Lee finished up.

They all nod their heads yes and then disperse. Frida, feeling embarrassed, approaches Lee.

"You didn't need to do that," she says, blushing.

"Yes, I did," Lee responds, placing her arms around her daughter-in-law's shoulders.

Franz is, in fact, treated like a prince. Lee soon furnishes one of the rooms in the house for him, who frequently is given new toys to complete his room.

Lee renovates another room for Frida and Heinz. Her daughter-in-law quickly learns about cotton cultivation and helps Lee administer the farm. Because she was a good student and avid reader, numbers come easily for Frida and, in little time, she's able to increase the farm's income.

Frida's been living with her mother-in-law for a month when the radio announces the end of the war, which is widely celebrated by everyone.

"He can come home now!" Frida tells Lee.

"Yes, we can look for him now," she replies.

The following morning, Frida see Lee writing many letters.

"Can I help you?" she asks.

"I'm finishing up," Lee responds. "I'm writing Heinz's commander and my brother… Maybe he's alive," she pauses. "And I'm also sending letters to friends of my husband, who might be able to help."

"Do you know Heinz's commander?" Frida asks.

"Yes, he fought alongside my late husband," she answers.

"Did you listen to the radio? They're arresting all the generals and high-ranking members of the Nazi Party… Maybe it would be better to look in the prisons," Frida says.

"We'll continue reading the newspapers. They'll tell us who was arrested," Lee says, sealing the letters. "I know my son. He wouldn't accept being a prisoner. He would've fled in time," she adds, trying to calm her.

Another month goes by. They've discovered nothing. They constantly scour the newspapers with the lists of the wounded, the dead, and prisoners looking for Heinz and Claus's name.

One Saturday morning, Frida finds Lee crying, while reading the newspaper. Her heart freezes and she can barely move.

After a few seconds of panic, Frida musters up enough courage to talk to her.

"What happened, Lee?" Frida asks, fearing the answer.

"Look... My brother..." Lee stammers. "His wife, too," Lee points out.

Frida takes the paper and reads that both of them had been sentenced to death. A chill runs up her spine and she begins to cry.

"Franz asked me to get his uncle and I thought he was already dead. It's my fault," Frida says, crying.

"No, it's not your fault," Lee states, also crying.

"I could have saved him, I could have," Frida blames herself.

"You had a child with you. You made the right decision. My brother would've been angry if you'd tried to rescue him," Lee pauses. "I know he's at peace now and would be happy that you and Franz are safe."

"I don't think I'll see my husband again," Frida says, anguished.

"I don't know what to think now, Frida," Lee replies, hugging her.

Frida and Lee's mutual respect and affection increase every day while hope of seeing Heinz fades.

The war had been over for 3 months and they no longer talked about Heinz. Both decided to start over and raise, to the best of their ability, little Franz, who was delighted by life on the farm.

Luckenwalde was now under Russian control and there were many rumors of rapes and mistreatment by the Russians. Lee constantly worried about their situation, particularly that of Frida, who was very pretty. Not wanting to affect the family's harmony, she kept her fears to herself.

Frida was helping her knit some socks when they observe an officer approaching in the distance. Lee, fearful, runs inside the house and grabs a shotgun, while Frida takes Franz from the garden and returns with a pistol.

Little by little, the officer approaches and both notice that he has a slight limp.

Frida then lowers the pistol and turns to Lee.

"Could it be him?" she asks, moving down a few steps from the house.

"Come back here, Frida. We need to be careful, no matter who it is," Lee says, standing next to her.

"Don't shoot!" the man shouts, limping and raising his hand. "I haven't crossed all of Germany just to get shot at home."

It was Heinz. Frida's heart almost burst out of her chest. Lee, overcome with emotion, faints, and Frida can't decide whether to help her mother-in-law or hug her husband.

"Great, now I think I've managed to kill my mother," Heinz says, smiling as he tries to approach. Seeing that Frida was still indecisive, he adds, "Frida, help my mother, please. I'm conscious."

She then bends over and tries to rouse her mother-in-law, who comes to.

"Are you okay, Mother? Are you sure?" Heinz asks, now beside her.

Lee nods her head yes and Frida then hugs and kisses Heinz.

"I'm okay, son!" Lee replies, now standing up.

"Can you help me now?" Heinz says, showing them a stomach wound.

None of the employees can restrain Franz any longer, who runs to his mother's side.

"Look, Franz, it's Daddy," Frida says excitedly. "Didn't I tell you he'd find us?"

Franz is totally happy, but shy; he hides behind his mother.

"Daddy?" inquires a confused Heinz, pointing at Franz.

"If you want, I'll explain in detail how he was made, in case you don't know," Frida says, laughing.

With difficulty, Heinz bends over and opens his arms for Franz, who runs to embrace him. Heinz's heart beats faster and he begins to laugh and cry at the same time.

"Mom, how many more of these do you have in there?" Heinz asks, smiling with his son on his arms.

"At the moment, only this one has shown up," Lee responds, slapping her son on the back.

"And what ugly name did your mother gave you?" Heinz asks Franz, joking.

"My name's pretty, I'm Franz," he says, grasping his father's neck.

"You named him after my father?" he asks, surprised, with tears in his eyes.

"Yes, your uncle adored him," Frida confirms.

"Mom, my uncle..." Heinz says, stammering.

"I know, dear. I saw it in the paper," Lee responds. "Let's take a look at that wound."

He had many cuts and scars, but no deep wounds. The following day, Heinz was better. He played with his son all day. It didn't seem like he'd been away for years to little Franz, who frolicked with his father until he got tired.

At lunch time, Frida calls both of them to eat. Heinz and Franz sit at the table together.

"Who made lunch?" Heinz asks.

"The cook," Lee replies. "Why?"

"I needed to know if I'd have to get a beer or not," Heinz says, chuckling.

Frida immediately understands the joke and punches her husband.

"What happened?" Lee asks, confused.

"I don't believe that Frida's cooked here yet," Heinz says, chortling.

Little Franz begins to laugh, too.

"Son, if you're laughing, I suspect you've eaten Mommy's food, right?" Heinz asks, smiling.

"I like Mommy's chocolate milk," Franz says.

"Dang, she learned to put chocolate in milk," Heinz says, chuckling. "You mother always boils milk to perfection," he adds, smiling.

"Don't you know how to cook, Frida?" Lee asks.

"I…" she tries to defend herself.

"Don't say that, Mom. I've already told you that she knows how to heat up milk. You've got to pay attention," Heinz says with a grin.

"I cook very well, mister! And Franz is alive," Frida says, laughing.

"I like Mommy. Don't fight with her," Franz declares, upset.

"I also like your mother, too, son… far from the kitchen," Heinz says, getting punched by Frida again.

After lunch, Heinz lays Franz down for his nap and calls both Frida and Lee to talk.

"I angered some people in France," Heinz says, beginning a serious conversation.

"The war's over. I sincerely don't want to know the details," Lee says to Heinz, standing up.

"Mom, I'm not going to give you details, but you need to listen," Heinz says.

Lee returns and sits down.

"I didn't come back sooner because I knew I was being watched," Heinz pauses. "I tried to get them to stop following me. I don't know how this Frenchman manage to get help from the Russians. I didn't think I'd ever see either of you again," he says, emotionally.

"It's all right dear. You managed and we're together," Frida states, taking Heinz's hand, which was shaking.

"You're all that matters to me in the world. I'm tired of fighting," Heinz says.

"I didn't want you entering that life. Your father warned you. We all warned you," Lee replies.

"Mom, I had to go... I wouldn't be able to forgive myself if I hadn't gone... and I never would have met Frida," Heinz says, kissing his wife's face.

"God's given you another chance. Take advantage of it," Lee says.

A week has gone by since Heinz's return, and every night he suffers from constant nightmares.

"I read about this in a book. It's normal for soldiers to have nightmares after a war. It's common trauma," Frida says, straightening Heinz's hair. He'd just had another nightmare and had woken up short of breath.

"That's not it, Frida. I've never had nightmares before," he responds.

"But it's normal. You saw many horrible things," Frida assures him.

"My father always told me that those who had nightmares had them because they were ashamed of what they'd done," Heinz pauses. "I'm not ashamed of what I did. Everything I did was done in the fairest and cleanest way a man of honor could do. I fought because I believed that I was doing so for my family and I'm not ashamed of that. Even if I was played for a fool, even if I participated indirectly in an unjustified killing, I didn't know it. My heart was at peace," Heinz added.

"Why?... Isn't your heart at peace now?"

"No... I have a son now. I don't want him to pay for my gullibility, for my ignorance," Heinz replies.

"What are you talking about... We're okay. Your son is happy here," Frida says.

"I know, which is why I feel bad saying this, but we need to flee," he states.

"What are you saying, Heinz. I'm sick of running. And who should we flee from? Or from what?" Frida asks, distressed.

"The Russians are going to find me. I know they will, and they won't spare you, or Franz, or even my mother," he says.

"Why won't they spare us? We're women and children. My father always said the army spares women and children, right?" Frida asks.

"They won't because Germany didn't spare their soldiers' women and children," Heinz replies.

"You're upsetting me. Either tell me everything or stop talking," Frida says, in anguish.

"They sent me out as a spy sometimes. I'm good at deciphering codes. I was ordered to discover and decode strategic enemy messages," Heinz pauses. "I discovered where a French lieutenant had hidden his family and I put it in my report. I never imagined they'd use that information, especially the way they did." Heinz pauses again. "But later, they arrested the lieutenant and tortured him, so he'd give information about the location of enemy troops. Because he wouldn't say anything, thanks to my analysis, in order soldiers could get the information they wanted, they captured his family. I found out later that they put the lieutenant face to face with his family and, as soon as he told them what they wanted to hear, they killed his family before his very eyes. The lieutenant was in our prison for months, and I visited him frequently, remorseful for my report. The lieutenant screamed in pain and cried, but he never heard me or even looked at me. When our troops were attacked, my lieutenant ordered our evacuation, and I learned that the French lieutenant was able to escape." Heinz puts his hand over his face. "I'm not responsible, and I don't feel responsible. I never imagined they'd do anything as shameful as that. But that French lieutenant blames me. He knows that I discovered where his family was. I have no doubt he wants revenge. The last time I met him, his eyes were burning with hatred. Nothing I said or did could change his opinion about me. So I fled!" Heinz says, crying.

"Do you think he'll find you here?" Frida asks.

"It's a matter of time," Heinz replies.

"Then we have to flee," Frida suggests. "We'll talk to your mother tomorrow."

"I'm also tired of fleeing," Heinz finishes, lying back down on the bed.

# Chapter XXIII

The next morning, everyone ate breakfast in silence and Heinz asked one of the kitchen helpers to take Heinz.

"Why can't I stay with Grandma, Daddy?" the boy asks.

"Grandma needs you to brush the horses. You love horses, don't you?" Heinz asks.

"The horseys are my friends," Franz states.

"Then your friends need to be brushed. Will you help them?" Lee says.

Franz, excited, leaves the room.

"What do you want to tell me, son?" Lee asks anxiously.

"Lee, we need to leave this house," Frida begins.

"I thought the three of us were living in harmony, but I'll understand if you want a home of your own," she says.

"That's not it. I like living with you. You're like a mother to me," Frida responds.

"We must leave this house, all of us," Heinz says, taking Lee's hand.

"But why, son? The war's over. You're not on the wanted list. I checked. Why do we need to leave?" Lee asks.

"I made some enemies, Mother, and they want revenge," Heinz says, lowering his head.

"Did you kill someone who didn't deserve to die?" Lee asks.

"In war, many die who don't deserve to, and many who do are alive. That's not the issue," Heinz explains, but Lee interrupts him.

"I'm asking if you did something you're ashamed of, or that you're remorseful about, like you father always asked?" Lee inquires.

"Mother, I did nothing that was not my duty as a soldier," Heinz responds.

"Did you serve at a concentration camp?" Lee further inquiries.

At this moment, Frida also becomes curious and worried. Both look at Heinz, who lowers his head.

"I discovered they existed when I read it in a newspaper. I spent a year in Italy and the rest in France, and no one ever told us anything. We just knew we were fighting for Germany and this is what I always told my subordinates," Heinz pauses. "I'm not ashamed of what I did. I'm ashamed of my ignorance, my lack of interest. I could have discovered things if I'd asked, but I never questioned them. I'm ashamed of what they did with the fruit of my labor."

"Why do we need to flee? I don't understand. You fulfilled your mission. You had nothing to do with what others did," Lee says.

"I, without knowing it, was responsible for a family being burnt to death," Heinz responds, with tears in his eyes.

"What do you mean, without knowing it? Did you accidently burn them?" Lee asks.

"No, Mom, I didn't. But the head of that family things it's my fault his family suffered, and now he wants revenge. Do you understand?" Heinz comments.

"Son, I only understand that you want to flee, and I'm too old for that," Lee says.

"I'm not going to leave you here," Heinz states. "We're all going to die, including your grandson, due to your stubbornness."

Heinz leaves the table, disturbed.

"Lee, he loves you so much and he's worried about you!" Frida says.

"I don't approve of fleeing. Neither did his father. I don't know where he came up with that idea," Lee replies, agitated. "A fugitive's life isn't life. It's pressure, stress, and fear of everything and everyone. You also shouldn't want that life for your son."

"Lee, he must think we're at a disadvantage," Frida says, trying to calm her.

"Frida, I know very well what's going through my son's head. He's afraid, because he now knows he has a son and knows how bad it is to grow up without a father. He would never have thought of fleeing before," Lee replies.

Heinz hadn't gone far and heard his mother's remarks.

"Dad never put his family at risk. I, without realizing it, did just that. That's the difference. I haven't lost my courage because of this," Heinz says, rather irritated.

"Son, use your head. If we flee, they'll hunt us for the rest of our lives. For me, that won't be long, but for you and Frida, it'll be a very long time," Lee responds.

Heinz sits down at the table again, calmer, and becomes pensive.

"You know I'm right!" Lee finishes up.

Frida's confused, in part because she agrees with Lee, but her fear of losing her family is also great.

"Mom, are you suggesting that I..." Heinz says, without finishing what he started.

"I'm not suggesting anything. I'm only asking that we not be fugitives, that you use your head," his mother replies.

Lee leaves both of them in the room, pensive, and departs the setting.

"What does she expect me... I mean... us to do," Heinz stammers.

"I think she just wants us to find a definitive solution to the problem," Frida says.

"She wants me to eliminate the problem... that's what she wants," Heinz states, agitated.

"You're no longer a soldier, and she knows that. We'd never ask that of you. Too many have died. You yourself said that many died for no reason at all," Frida says, in a serious tone.

"I just know one way to solve this problem definitively," Heinz responds.

"If your only idea is to dirty your hands with more blood, I won't help you. I've already dirtied mine too much," she states angrily.

"You've changed," Heinz says.

"I haven't changed. I've suffered. That's different. I don't want our son to have to go through anything equal or similar to our situation, and that's why I don't want him to see this kind of violence. If we're lucky, he'll forget what he's seen already," Frida replies.

"Do you have another idea in mind to solve our problem," Heinz asks.

"Why do men always need to solve everything with violence? Violence creates violence, and that's why we're in this mess," Frida replies.

"What are you suggesting? I'm still waiting for an answer," Heinz says.

"My idea will be difficult and it's extremely crazy, too, but if it works, no one will get hurt and we'll solve the problem definitively."

"Did you see this brilliant idea in some book?" he inquires.

"No, this idea came from a mother who understands the rage of losing her family," Frida responds.

Lee returns with Franz and a glass of milk.

"Have you come to a decision," Lee asks.

"We're not going to flee," Frida confirms.

"I don't remember having agreed to this decision…" Heinz says.

# Chapter XXIV

Three weeks have passed. The Fritz family sleeps with one eye open.

"Your idea's insane," Heinz says.

"Do you have any other suggestion?" Frida asks. "The cook told me that Russian troops are asking about us in the city. We don't have much time for new ideas."

"I'll tell everyone working on the farm to leave tomorrow. We'll have to work hard, but it'll be better if they aren't here," he says.

"Work isn't a problem, but you're right. The fewer lives we put at risk, the better," Frida agrees.

Lee returns from downtown rather agitated.

"Russian troops are everywhere. Families are fleeing to the American lines… The city is in a state of chaos; I couldn't buy anything," she says.

"The Russians are ruthless," Heinz affirms.

"It's like another war," Lee says.

"Do you think they're creating all this chaos because of us?" Frida asks.

"I don't think we're responsible for an entire battalion of Russian troops being in the city. The Frenchman's influential, but he isn't that influential," Heinz responds.

"I agree with Heinz; I think they're just showing their power," Lee says.

"If there are large numbers of Russians, they'll find us soon," Frida states.

"But we're not hiding. Wasn't that your plan?" Lee questions.

"Thanks to you two, we're not hiding. I want to make that clear," Heinz says.

They all went to bed apprehensive that night, except for little Franz, who slept peacefully.

The next day was rather agitated for the Fritz family. Taking care of the farm by themselves proved to be harder than they'd imagined.

That night, Fritz and Heinz took turns keeping watch.

It was late at night when she saw the headlights from two cars in the distance, which was suspicious at that time of night. She runs to the room and wakes Heinz and Lee up. They were sleeping in their clothes.

"Over there. It's looks like they were waiting for us," one of the Russian soldiers comments in English, observing the family that had lined up in front of the house with their hands raised.

A lieutenant wearing a uniform exits the second car.

"Heinz Fritz, you're a difficult man to find," says the lieutenant. "The people in town said you have a son.

Where's the little brat?" the lieutenant completes in French-accented English.

"I thought you'd spare my son, because of how much you've suffered,"

"You spared neither my son, nor my two daughters. Not even my wife," the lieutenant says in a rage.

"I'd never have had the stomach to touch your family. I've already told you that. I wasn't even in the same city; you were there and saw it all," Heinz states.

"You did nothing to defend them," the lieutenant says.

"There was nothing I could do," Heinz justifies.

"Why did you give them my family's address? What did that add?" the lieutenant asks.

"They asked me to list all relatives' addresses, and they told me it was so they could inform them if the prisoner was executed. That's why I listed it. I thought it was right for your family to know what happened to you. I never imagined it'd put them at risk," Heinz says.

"You German piece of shit. Heartless Nazi. Do you expect me to believe you thought your friends would send flowers after killing a prisoner? What kind of imbecile would believe that?" the lieutenant inquires.

"I'm guilty of being an imbecile, that's true, but I did not kill your family," Heinz says.

"Do you think I'm going to shake your hand and say everything's fine now?" the lieutenant asks.

"Tell me how to resolve this impasse. If I'd helped your family, they would've killed mine. And now you want to kill them, but they've done nothing. Either way, innocent families died, and now you want that killing to continue. Is that it?" Heinz asks.

"Don't worry. Your family will be the last innocents to die. Go inside and bring out his son. Kill anyone who tries to stop you," the lieutenant orders.

"There's no one in there but us and, if you allow me, I'll bring out my son; he'll be very frightened if a soldier gets him," Frida says.

"He'll be even more frightened by what I'm going to do to you. We can wait," the lieutenant responded, with rage in his eyes. "But you two stay right where you are. Somebody goes in with the young woman."

Everyone returns to the front of the house and Frida carries little Franz, who, frightened, says nothing.

"If it's justice you want, be just and take my son," Heinz says.

"I want you to watch him die, just like I watched my children die!" the lieutenant states.

"Okay, I'm tired of arguing with you. Maybe your justice will end our suffering. I'm tired of living with your senseless rage," Heinz says.

"That German soldier thinks he's going to be a martyr!" one of the Russian soldiers says.

"Can I have a little fun with his wife?" asks one of the Russian soldiers. "She's pretty."

"We didn't do that to your wife or daughters. Be fair!" Heinz says, stepping in front of Frida.

"He's right, they didn't," the lieutenant agrees.

"Let's just get this over with once and for all," Heinz says. "Tie my family up in the house and set everything on fire! Isn't that what they did to your family? Isn't that what you want to do to me?" Heinz provokes.

"Why do you want to die, Heinz?" the lieutenant asks, suspecting something.

"I've had it with all this fighting. I can't sleep at night thinking about what might have been. I've been a weakling for not having already killed myself like my commanders did, those who had the chance. To live in a world without Hitler, without Nazism? We have no future and you'll be doing us a favor by killing us!" Heinz replies, lying.

"How can you think that Hitler was a hero? You Nazi monster!" the lieutenant asks.

"Because Nazism was a cure for a sick world..." Heinz continues with his lie, realizing that, little by little, the lieutenant was giving in.

"Fine, I'll do you a favor. I'll be more noble than you were with my family that didn't want to die," the lieutenant says. "No one touches his wife. Let's tie them up."

Heinz follows the lieutenant, who places three chairs in the center of the living room.

"Sit down!" the lieutenant orders.

"There's no chair for my son," Frida says.

"Put him on your lap. That way, Heinz will have a better view of him burning," the lieutenant says, chuckling. "Search those two before you tie them up!"

"What about the kid and the old woman?" one of the Russian soldiers asks.

"The brat can't do anything, and the old woman can barely stand up. Can't you see that?" the lieutenant replies.

Lee walked slowly, pretending she was in pain all over.

After being searched, Frida and Heinz are tied, one in front of the other. Franz is then placed on his mother's lap with his feet and hands tied. Lee is the last one to be tied up.

"Burn everything!" the lieutenant orders, smirking as he leaves the house.

The Russian soldiers pour gasoline all over the house and the fire immediately roars.

Heinz waits for the last soldier to leave and signals to Frida.

"Let's go, Franz. Get up!" she says.

Over the last few days, Franz had been practicing with his father how to escape when he was tied. Heinz knew his son's knots would be the loosest.

Franz quickly slips out of the rope binding him and hands his father the knife he was hiding in his pants. Heinz then unties his family and asks everyone to scream in agony.

After a few screams, Heinz pulls the carpet in the room where, previously, he'd dug a tunnel with the help of the workers. In the tunnel, with Frida's help, he removes the decomposing bodies of three adults and a child they'd removed from an abandoned concentration camp near the city and hidden in the tunnel a few days earlier.

Once the bodies had been put into position, everyone enters the tunnel and Heinz puts the tunnel's cover back in place.

The passageway leads the family to the stable near the house. There, Frida had hidden all the family's money, some clothes and a car, that had taken the place of the animals they'd sold.

Heinz knew the lieutenant would watch the house until it had completely burned, as had happened to his family. With this in mind, they waited until everyone left the farm and silence returned to the place.

It was past three in the morning when everyone left the farm.

"And now?" Heinz asks, looking at Frida.

"What do you mean? Don't you know?" Lee asks.

"She made me responsible for getting us killed, saying she'd do the rest," Heinz replied.

Everyone looks at Frida, who says, "And now we'll go to the port," Frida replies.

"What will we do at the port?" Lee queries.

"We're going to start over," Frida responds, getting into the car with Franz.

"I don't want to go on a trip, Mommy!" Franz says.

"This one will be different, son. Daddy will be with us," Frida says, stroking her son's hair.

They all get into the car.

# Chapter XXV

Once at the port, Frida goes to the ticket counter alone while Heinz sells the car, following Frida's instructions.

"Where are we going?" Lee asks.

"We're going somewhere we can live in peace!"

They all embark, and the captain orders the lines cast off.

"Ladies and gentlemen, we expect this to be a safe trip to our destination on the Thames River in London," the captain announces in English.

"You're taking me to England?" Lee asks.

"Yes, and from this point on, we should speak English," Frida emphasizes.

"But I don't speak English very well," Lee says.

"Your son knows how to take care of that problem," Frida replies, smiling.

"From this point on, you've lost your voice, Mom," Heinz says, chuckling.

After explaining everything, the Fritz family tries to enjoy the voyage.

On the Thames River, all passengers are subjected to a minor inspection by British soldiers because the ship had arrived from Germany.

"What are you doing in London?" asks the soldier in German.

"Would you speak English, please?" Frida asks.

"What are you doing on a ship from Germany?" the soldier asks.

"I was held prisoner in there. We were only freed recently," she replies.

"Why did they arrest your family?" asks the soldier.

"They only arrested me. I met the other two in prison and the child was born in prison," Frida responds.

"And why did they arrest you? Were you a soldier?" asks the soldier, smiling.

"They arrested me because I am the daughter of Col. John Myer. My name is Jane Myer and I demand respect. My father was killed in action, alongside my mother. I am the sole survivor," Jane replies.

"If you are a member of the Myer family, where is your identification?" asks the soldier, doubting Jane.

For the Royal Army, Col. Myer had died a hero and his family had died with him, according to British newspapers, which is why the soldier was scornful, doubting Jane.

"I was held prisoner for years. Do you think they let me keep my identification? All I have is this ring with the family coat of arms. Now tell me whether you recognize it or not?" Jane replies, showing the ring that had never left her finger.

"I... I," stammers the soldier.

"Before I lose my patience with you, do your duty as a soldier and call your superior officer. I'll speak with him," she says angrily.

Lee, Franz, and Heinz observe Jane without saying anything. Heinz, particularly, is startled by her pluck, which he had never seen before.

A few minutes later, a sergeant appears.

"Are you the young woman who says is a Myer?" asks the sergeant.

"I'm not just saying that. I am a Myer!" responds Jane. "Is Col. Daniel Stuart still alive?" inquires Jane.

"And what do you want with Col. Stuart?" the sergeant says.

"It so happens that he fought alongside my father and is my godfather. Call him and let me go home."

The sergeant makes the call and immediately releases Jane and her family.

"Excuse me, Miss Myer, I didn't realize there was a Myer still alive. We thought you had all died," the sergeant confirms, stammering. "Your godfather asked us to take you to a hotel where he'll visit you. Please, follow me. I'll take you there personally," says the sergeant, looking down.

At the hotel's reception desk, they ask everyone's name.

"I'm Jane, this is my husband Edward, my son Franz, and my mother-in-law Evelyn," Jane replies.

Upon entering their room, Edward, confused, asks, "Why Edward?".

"Why Frida?" Jane inquires, for the very first time.

"Because it was the first name that came to my head under pressure," Edward says.

"Ditto," says Jane, smiling.

"And why Evelyn?" Evelyn asks.

"It's your name in English," Jane responds. "I just kept my son's name because all of this name changing will be confusing for a child."

Jane's godfather arrives a few hours later and, upon seeing Jane, embraces her affectionately.

"Jane, I thought you were dead," Daniel says, with tears in his eyes.

"I almost died, but my husband saved me," responds Jane, pointing to Edward.

"Your father made a will leaving everything to you. Since they couldn't confirm your death because they didn't find your body, I've managed to keep the will unopened. I'm happy you're alive," Daniel says. "The little princess Myer is now a mother; your father would be proud of your strength."

"Thanks! Have you sold the house?" Jane asks.

"No, I haven't. I left Nana in charge of it. She suffered greatly when she heard you'd been killed," Daniel responds.

"Dear Nana, how I miss her!" says Jane, with tears in her eyes. "I'm going home," she adds.

Jane stays in London for a few days to take care of the paperwork from the will and to legally give her last name to everyone in the family.

"Officially, you are all now Myers! My father, wherever he is, must be happy knowing he now has a son," Jane says happily.

The following day, she returns home. Nana is waiting in front of the house.

"My Jane!" Nana exclaims, crying with her arms open.

Jane runs to Nana and both of them embrace, crying.

"And you're still running, aren't you, my child?" Nana asks.

"And you're still taking care of me," Jane says.

The rest of the family approaches Nana.

"Nana, I want you to help me take care of my son just like you did me. This is Franz, and this is my husband Edward and my mother-in-law Evelyn," Jane says, without releasing Nana.

"It'll be a pleasure caring for this boy. He's the most beautiful thing in the world!" Nana responds, hugging Franz, who, being a charmer, kisses her cheek. "Let's go through your mother's toys in the basement. I think there's something for you there!" she adds, picking Franz up.

"My, what a lovely house, what a marvelous garden," Evelyn exclaims.

"Now we're free to be happy!" Edward confirms, kissing her.

Franz returns with a ball and plays with his father and Nana in the garden. Evelyn rushes to see the house.

Jane walks in the garden and finds the bench where she often observed her parents sitting, holding hands, watching the sun set.

The sun was now going down. Jane bends over in front of the bench and digs a hole in the ground with her hands. She kisses her mother's ring on her hand and buries it.

Jane sits by herself on the bend and watches the sunset. Edward observes Jane in the distance and decides to join her.

"Do you regret something, Jane?" Edward asks.

"I regret switching the salt and sugar in that cake. I don't think you'll ever forget that," Jane says, smiling.

"Never," Edward replies, laughing. "Let's go in. It's getting dark!"

"Go on yourself. I'll come in a bit," Jane says.

Edward realizes Jane wants to be alone for a bit longer and goes inside with Nana and Franz.

"Mum, Dad, wherever you are, forgive me for not being able to save you," Jane pauses. "But thank you for having saved me."

Jane stands up and looks at the bench again.

"Thank you for taking me on the most frightening and happy journey of my life."

Printed in Great Britain
by Amazon